Return
to the
Secret
Garden

First published in the UK
in 2015 by Scholastic Children's Books
An imprint of Scholastic Ltd
Euston House, 24 Eversholt Street
London, NW1 1DB, UK
Registered office: Westfield Road, Southam,
Warwickshire, CV47 0RA
SCHOLASTIC and associated logos are trademarks
and/or registered trademarks of Scholastic Inc.

ISBN 978 1407 16445 8

A CIP catalogue record for this work is available from the
British Library.

Printed and bound by CPI Group (UK) Ltd,
Croydon, CR0 4YY
Papers used by Scholastic Children's Books are made from wood grown
in sustainable forests.

3 5 7 9 10 8 6 4 2

www.scholastic.co.uk

www.holly-webb.com

SCHOLASTIC

Return
to the
Secret
Garden

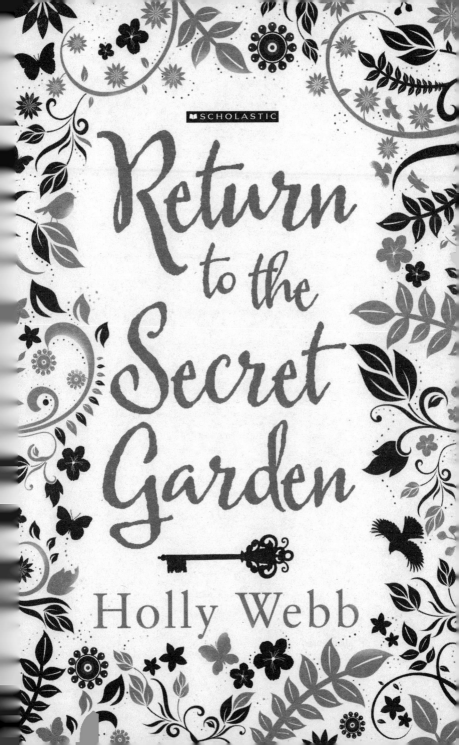

Holly Webb

For my mother

Chapter One

The children marched down the street in a crocodile, and only one of them looked back. The others didn't turn, because they didn't need to. There was nothing to look back for. Everything they owned was with them — a few clothes, here and there a battered, shapeless stuffed toy. Each of them carried a paper parcel, and a gas mask, and that was all they had.

Emmie trailed, peering over her shoulder, so that Arthur behind her gave her a shove to tell her to keep up. She kicked him, swiftly, and walked backwards instead, still trying to see.

But Lucy wasn't there. It was stupid to expect that she would be, anyway, Emmie thought. Lucy hardly ever came out on to the street — she was shy, and she hated loud noises. Emmie still stared, though, hoping to see the small black cat peering after her round the corner of the tall house. Lucy had probably fled out into the backyard, Emmie decided miserably, and she kicked Arthur again, because he was smirking at her, and because she felt like it.

"Emmeline Hatton!"

Emmie whipped round with a sigh. Of course Miss Dearlove hadn't seen Arthur giving her a push. She never did see. "Me, Miss?" she asked innocently, trying to look as though she didn't know what was the matter.

The matron glared at her. "No, the other Emmeline Hatton. Of course you! You bad-tempered little girl, how dare you kick Arthur like that?"

"He pushed me..." Emmie started to say, but Miss Dearlove didn't bother to listen; she grabbed Emmie by the arm and hauled her up to the front of the line. She was a tiny little lady, not actually much bigger than Emmie, but Emmie didn't dare pull away. She had known Miss Dearlove for ever. The matron was like a busy little clockwork train, wound up into a clicking fuss of pure crossness. It was best not to get in her way – but somehow Emmie always did.

"You can walk here with Miss Rose and the

babies, since you can't be trusted to behave like a ten-year-old. Why is it always you? And after your ridiculous behaviour this morning as well. As if we haven't got enough to worry about." She glanced down at her watch. "Miss Rose, we need to hurry; the station's bound to be busy, and there isn't that much time to spare." She scuttled down to the end of the line again, with one last hissed "Behave!" to Emmie.

Miss Rose was usually less bad-tempered than the matron, but even she eyed Emmie and sighed. "Today, of all days, Emmie? I would have thought you'd have more sense."

"He shoved me," Emmie muttered. She knew it wasn't quite true, but she wasn't letting them have the last word. "It isn't fair. Why do I always get into trouble?" She walked down the street next to Miss Rose, seething and muttering to herself. If she huffed and growled, she wouldn't cry, and she wasn't going to give Arthur Banks the satisfaction of that, however much Miss Rose frowned.

They had been told the day before that they were going. Miss Dearlove had stood up at the end of breakfast, and explained that since war was expected to be declared within a few days, the

Craven Home for Orphaned Children would be evacuated "somewhere safe".

No one knew what evacuation meant, except that it was vaguely connected with the rows of brown boxes on the shelves in the schoolroom, which had the gas masks in. Once a week for the last few months they had pulled them on, and sat staring at each other, snout-nosed and goggle-eyed. After the first few tries, Arthur had worked out how to make a rude noise, a sort of farting snort around the rubber face piece. He did it every time now, and they all laughed – even Miss Dearlove didn't sound that cross when she told him off.

But Emmie had dreamed of those huge round eyes almost every night since. The glass lenses of the masks leaned over her, stooping down close, and staring. The gas masks were supposed to help them breathe, Miss Dearlove said, but when Emmie thought of her mask, sealed away in its flimsy cardboard box, she found her breath catching in her throat. Where was this gas going to come from anyway? No one had said. Arthur and his mate Joey said that it would be dropped by planes, but all the gas that Emmie knew of came in pipes, to the kitchen for the stoves. She didn't see how it could be carried in a plane. If only someone would explain, she thought bitterly, kicking at a crack in the pavement as they marched on. Where were they going, and why? What was happening? No one told them anything. They didn't need to know, they just got parcelled up like their clothes and sent away...

"Look." The little girl Emmie had been shoved in next to tugged at her sleeve.

"What?" Emmie muttered, not looking.

"Over there." Ruby pointed across the road. "See, Emmie, there! Do you think they're being evacuated too?"

Emmie turned, and saw that they were passing a school, where a long column of children were lining up in the playground. They were carrying an assortment of battered cases and brown paper parcels, and there were labels tied on to their coats.

"I suppose so."

"Just like us..." Ruby said thoughtfully. "I didn't know everybody was."

"We have to get out of the cities – in case of planes flying over," Emmie said vaguely. "All the children do." That was what the boys had thought, anyway. They had been lurking about the matrons' sitting room, listening to the news broadcasts, so she supposed it was possible they were right. The children in the playground did look quite like them, except that there were mothers huddling around them, and even a few fathers. They were pushing packets of sandwiches into children's pockets, hugging them, running along beside them as the line of children started to snake out on to the street. The children marched away, following two older boys, who had a banner with the school's name stitched on to it – almost like a procession, Emmie thought.

Some of the school children were crying, Emmie noticed. A lot of the smaller ones were clinging on to their mothers, pale-faced and bewildered. They didn't seem to know what was happening either. But some of the others looked happy, swinging their cases as if they were off on holiday. Perhaps they were – they might end up at the seaside.

Emmie blinked thoughtfully. She was almost sure that she'd never been out of London. Until now, she hadn't really thought about where they were going; she'd been too worried about what they were leaving behind. Maybe those two boys in the line grinning all over their faces were right. It was an adventure. . .

But almost all the mothers were brushing tears

away, quickly, with the sides of their hands so as not to show. Emmie shivered. She supposed the children from the Home were lucky – all the adults they knew were coming with them. It didn't make her feel lucky though. She tried to remember the softness of Lucy's head bumping against her fingers, the warmth of her breath as the little cat nuzzled against her. But all she could hear was Ruby, grizzling because she was tired, and her shoes were too tight.

They hadn't gone all that far, but the streets were so much busier than the quiet area around the Craven Home. Even Emmie felt tired, with so many people pressing around her, and the constant roar of cars and carts and buses along the bustling street. On any other day, it would have been fun to stand on one of those islands in the road and watch, and wonder where all these people were streaming off to. Today, Emmie wished she was back sitting in the window of her dormitory, peering out at the street for the grocer's van, and a car every so often. She'd wished for something to happen, something exciting, and now it had.

"We're almost there, Ruby," Miss Rose said soothingly. "The station's just along the road there, do you see – the clock tower, and the name underneath. King's Cross."

The station was huge, with two great curving arched windows across the front, like tunnel mouths.

"London and North Eastern Railway? Are we going north-east, then, Miss?" Emmie demanded curiously, looking at the rest of the white letters along the roof. But Miss Rose ignored her, starting to chivvy the line of children across the road. A policeman waved them over, holding up a line of buses, and smiling down at little Ruby, clutching her faded bear.

There were other lines of children converging on the station now, hundreds of them, marching along like little ants. More and more poured out of buses, labelled, carrying parcels and bags and battered cases. Emmie had never seen so many people her own age before. How many were going out of London?

Miss Rose slowed as she walked them past the scattering of shops around the front of the great building, and glanced round anxiously for Miss Dearlove.

"What is it?" Emmie asked. Miss Rose looked so

suddenly uncertain. All the staff at the Home had been brisk and decided about the move, brushing away questions and hurrying the children over their meagre packing. Now, for the first time, Emmie wondered if they were as confused and worried as the children. Mrs Evans the cook was clutching her big black handbag against her front like a shield.

"Nothing, Emmie!" Miss Rose said, sharply for her. She was glancing between the sandbags built up around the doorway, and a flight of steps down – still signed to the Underground, but blocked off with a great pile of bits of broken stone. She glanced down at Emmie, with a bright smile that showed her teeth. "I just wasn't quite sure which door we were to take, that's all. We must expect everything to look a little different in wartime, mustn't we?" she added in a comforting, sing-song voice, as though Emmie had been the one to be scared.

Miss Rose didn't allow herself to be daunted by the huge space inside the station, or the milling crowd of children. She straightened her shoulders and marched them in, then started counting everybody again in case one of the twenty orphans had disappeared on the way. Emmie didn't think that any of them would have dared. Not with those planes coming, and the gas. She had thought about running away before – on days when nothing happened, and no one spoke to her. But that had been before she found Lucy.

Miss Dearlove marched over to a man in station uniform, and he frowned down at his list, and eventually pointed across to one of the furthest platforms – and then he checked his watch, and pointed again, flapping his hands.

The matron came trotting back to them, and caught Emmie's hand, pulling at her sharply. "We haven't much time – come along, all of you. No dawdling. There are so many extra trains for the evacuated schools," she added to Miss Rose. "The timetable is all upset. If we miss this one, we'll have to wait hours." She glanced irritably down at Emmie as she said it – it was her fault that they were late, after all.

The train was already steaming as the children hurtled on to the platform, and a porter flung the doors open for them, bundling them in as Miss Rose and Miss Dearlove and Mrs Evans wrestled with bags and food baskets.

Emmie collapsed on to a padded seat, clutching her brown paper parcel of clothes, and stared out of the window – she could see another train in the next platform, with a girl gazing back at her. She smiled faintly, recognizing the strange girl's expression of fear, and excitement. There was even something of her own sickening loneliness. Perhaps that girl had never been out of London either. Perhaps she'd never been on a train. But maybe, just perhaps, the train was taking her towards something new and different. Things might be better – even though she'd had to leave so much behind.

The girl waved at her, and Emmie lifted her hand, slowly, as their train shuddered and creaked, and began to pull out of the station, out of London, making for somewhere else.

Emmie leaned back against the scratchy velour of the seat. She was facing the window, but she was hardly looking at the green banks of the cutting that the train was racing through. She wondered where that other girl's train had been going. She had looked nice – no, not nice. Nice was what Miss Dearlove and Miss Rose were always encouraging them to be. *Play nicely. Now, that isn't nice, is it, Emmie? Nice little girls don't behave like that.*

The only other girl Emmie's age at the Craven

Home had left when they were both about five. Louisa had been very nice indeed, and that was why she had been adopted. It had been made quite clear to Emmie that if only she had been more like Louisa, she might have been adopted too. But she was much too old for that now. And she didn't care anyway.

Emmie ran her hand over the arm of the seat, and tears stung the corners of her eyes. The dark, dusty stuff reminded her of Lucy's fur.

Whenever one of the younger, sweeter, *nicer* children was taken away to have a proper home, or when Miss Dearlove snapped at her for being ungrateful, or the boys teased her for being skinny and pale and ugly, Emmie would simply shrug and stare. Miss Dearlove called her insolent, and Arthur had boxed her ears for *giving him that look*.

She'd stare, until Miss Dearlove flounced away, or the boys grew bored. And then she'd sneak upstairs, to the little window on the landing outside the girls' dormitory. There was a great cupboard half in front of it, full of musty blankets, and spare clothes, and a skinny, ugly little person could squeeze behind the cupboard, and open the window – and climb out on to the rusted iron fire escape without anyone knowing where she had gone.

For the first few times Emmie had been out there, in the days just after she found the window, she'd sat there alone, gazing out across the roofs below. She loved the view – watching the clouds streaked with red as the sun went down. Even on the days when London was choked in fog, she had imagined the sky, and the rooftops, beneath the layers of grey. If she leaned against the railings, she could just see a slice of the road, and watch for passers-by, and wonder where they were going, and where she would go, one day. She'd even taken a few steps down the fragile old metal staircase. But then common sense had sent her slinking back again. She had nowhere to go. She couldn't leave.

Emmie had been out on the fire escape on a February afternoon when she first saw her. It had been almost dark, and icy cold, especially as she hadn't a coat. She couldn't sneak her coat upstairs, not without someone stopping to ask her why. But being cold was worth it, for time alone to think, and watch the sky.

Emmie had felt as though she was all alone in the city. A purplish light had soaked through the sky, and wisps of cloud floated by, looking almost close enough to touch. Emmie leaned against the metal railings, feeling the hard cold of the iron bite into her cheek, and knowing she should go in, before they missed her.

Something had made her stay. Afterwards she thought she'd known something was going to happen. There was the faintest creaking on the metal steps, and a darker patch of shadow slunk on to the tiny landing where Emmie was curled.

"A cat!" she whispered. The cat was tiny – hardly more than a kitten – and shy. It hesitated at the edge of the landing, watching her suspiciously. She caught a gleam of light reflected in its eyes. Why had it come all the way up here?

Emmie moved her hand cautiously towards her pocket, trying not to move suddenly and scare the cat away. She had hidden a sandwich in her handkerchief – fish paste. She hated it, and they were supposed to finish everything that was on their plates. Usually she dropped the scraps off the fire escape, but she'd forgotten. She held back a laugh. Perhaps this cat had eaten her leftovers before. Perhaps that was why it had come.

She opened out her handkerchief, and wrinkled her nose at the smell. But there was a scuffling in the darkness; the cat had moved. It could smell the fish paste too. Someone turned on the light inside and both Emmie and the cat froze. But no one saw the open window. There was a quick patter of footsteps up the stairs, and one of the little girls disappeared into the dormitory.

With the light on, Emmie could see the cat, tiny and skinny – like her. It was hunched at the corner of the metal floor, eyes fixed on the half-unwrapped sandwich, but too scared to come closer.

Slowly, Emmie put the handkerchief down between them, and unfolded it properly, to let the little thing have a glimpse of the food. Then she wriggled further back against the wall of the house.

"You may as well eat it," she whispered. "I won't. You can have it." She watched the cat curiously – it was nothing like the cats she had seen in the schoolroom books. They were plump and cushiony, with long white whiskers. This creature looked half-starved – and it couldn't resist the sandwich for long. It darted forward and began to tear at the bread, glancing over at Emmie every so often, to check that she wasn't moving.

When the sandwich was gone, the cat sniffed at the handkerchief, and even licked it, as if the flavour of the fish paste had soaked into the cotton.

Then it turned and whisked away, skinny tail held low, and Emmie leaned over to watch it scurry down the steps.

The next night, she had only bread and butter, but the cat didn't seem to mind. It ate the whole slice, and then when Emmie held out her fingers, it sniffed them curiously before it darted away.

Emmie kept taking her scraps out to the fire escape, and the cat kept turning up. As soon as she climbed out of the window, a small dark shape would appear, faster and faster each time. There were days she couldn't get out, of course, days when Miss Dearlove decided on a "brisk walk" or the inspectors came. But it only took seconds for Emmie to slip behind the cupboard and open the window a crack, and drop her scraps out on to the fire escape.

It was an odd feeling, waiting and hoping for a glimpse of black fur. It wasn't even as if the cat stayed for long, not for those first few days, anyway. She – Emmie was only guessing it was a she, but "it" all the time sounded mean – would eat whatever Emmie had brought, and then when she was sure that all the food was gone, she would hurry off back to whatever it was she had been doing. Sniffing around the bins, probably, Emmie thought.

It seemed strange to mind so much, to sit in lessons and hope that she would turn up, but Emmie found that she thought about the cat more than she thought of anything else. She had never had a pet, or known any sort of animal. The Craven Home only had the occasional mouse, and then only in the kitchens, where the children weren't really supposed to go. There wasn't any chance of taming a mouse with crumbs, even if Emmie had wanted to. Knowing that the cat came to see her, or her sandwiches, tugged at something inside Emmie. The cat wanted her, even if it was only for food. It needed her – and she needed it too.

In the third week, the cat climbed into Emmie's lap when she wasn't fast enough unwrapping another fish-paste sandwich, and Emmie named her Lucy.

"Emmie! Emmie!" Someone pulled at her hand, and Emmie realized Ruby was talking to her.

"Don't you want a sandwich?" Ruby pushed one into her hand, and Emmie stared down at it, trying not to gag. It was fish paste.

"No!" she said sharply, and shoved it back at Ruby. Then she caught Miss Rose's eye, and added, "No, thank you. I'm not hungry."

"There's plain bread and butter, Emmie." Miss Rose passed her another paper packet. "You need to eat something; it'll be hours more yet. It's a long way," she went on gently.

Emmie nodded. She was too miserable even to ask again where they were going, in case she started to cry.

"Missing that scrawny cat?" Joey leaned over, speaking through a mouthful of sandwich, and Emmie pressed herself back against the seat disgustedly. If only they hadn't all seen. She had kept Lucy a secret for weeks, but the little cat grew tamer and a tiny bit plumper, and she was clever enough to work out that Emmie – and more food – were inside the house.

Miss Dearlove shooed her out, but Miss Rose seemed to like cats. When she saw Lucy sitting on a windowsill, or sneaking along the passage by the schoolroom, she smiled faintly and looked the other way instead of chasing the little cat outside again. And the cook liked her – Lucy had the sense to catch a mouse and drop it in front of Mrs Evans's feet. After that, Emmie would occasionally see a saucer of milk in the yard at the bottom of the fire escape – a saucer where there had once been milk, anyway.

How could they have made her leave Lucy behind, if what everyone said was true, and London was going to be flattened by bombs? And the gas. Emmie had heard Miss Rose and the cook saying that all the post boxes were being painted with special gas-detecting paint, so they'd glow yellow instead of red if there was gas floating in the streets. It sounded as though it was going to happen any day now. What would happen to Lucy, if that was real?

She shivered, and closed her eyes for a second. She could see Lucy lying on the little iron landing of the fire escape, basking in the sun. The little cat liked to stretch out on her side, showing off her rusty reddish-black underneath – sometimes she even lay on her back, with her paws in the air. She'd wave them, as if she was inviting Emmie to rub the fluff of her belly – and then if Emmie dared, half the time Lucy would pounce on her, and worry her wrist. But Emmie didn't mind the scratches.

The other children had petted Lucy, and even fed her scraps, but she seemed to remember that Emmie had been her first protector – and she always came back to the fire escape.

Emmie had found a basket the night before,

while they were packing. It was in that same cupboard of odds and ends that stood in front of their window. There must have been a cat once before – or perhaps it was meant for picnics in the park, although Emmie wasn't sure anyone at the Home had ever done something so lovely. She hadn't asked Miss Dearlove or Miss Rose if they could take the cat – she hadn't even thought about it. It had been so clear to her that Lucy could not be left behind. She'd simply been grateful that she wouldn't have to carry Lucy in her arms, or tie a string around her neck. She didn't think the cat would like being on a train.

But before breakfast wasn't Lucy's time to appear slinking through the kitchen, or creeping up to the top of the iron staircase. Emmie had lain awake half the night, worrying about it. She'd have to go out into the yard and call the cat, she decided. If Lucy thought there was extra food in it for her, she'd come. Perhaps she could nick something from the kitchen to tempt her with.

Emmie flung on her clothes as soon as the bell rang. She grabbed the basket from under her bed, and hurried through the press of twenty excited, bewildered children, dropping paper parcels and gas masks and winter coats that smelled of mothballs – because even though it was a sweltering September day, who knew how long they'd be away for?

The cook was trying to get breakfast, and pack up sandwiches, and tidy the kitchen all at once. It was simple enough to sneak past her into the larder, and snatch the dripping jar. That would smell good, Emmie thought, dripping, since she couldn't find any fish. She stood under the fire escape, cooing and clucking to call Lucy in, waving the jar.

Miss Dearlove raced about, spooning porridge into the little ones, sewing back on buttons, and in between, dashing back into the kitchen to screech at Mrs Evans the cook about twenty sets of sandwiches.

In the passage outside the kitchen, she came on Emmie, with a fingerful of beef dripping, trying to persuade Lucy into the lidded basket. The little cat had her front paws in, and Emmie was wondering if she should just take a chance and shove the rest of her in too.

"Emmie! For pity's sake, why haven't you got your coat on? We're about to leave! What's in that basket – you've not put your clothes in there, have you? You should have them in a parcel, like the others."

Emmie glanced round at her, and Miss Dearlove sucked in her cheeks.

Lucy saw that Emmie was distracted, and took her chance to launch out of the basket.

"No!" Emmie squeaked. "Oh, Miss, catch her!" And she flung herself full length, grabbing the thin black cat – who to Miss Dearlove looked just as scruffy and ugly as the little girl. Emmie was sallow-skinned, and thinner than ever, since she'd been hiding away half her food to feed the cat. Her hair had wisped its way out of her thin plaits already, and her arms were all scratched.

"That disgusting stray! I might have known. . ." Then the matron stopped, and stared at the basket. "Emmie Hatton, did you think you were taking that creature with you?"

Emmie crawled clumsily on to her knees, and stood up slowly, gripping the squirming cat in her arms. She stood there, wincing as Lucy flailed her claws and pulled several more threads out of her cardigan. The cat didn't care that she was being saved; she was hungry, and she had not liked the basket at all.

"We have to," she whispered, her greenish eyes widening as she stared back at Miss Dearlove. It wasn't one of her purposeful stares – she wasn't trying to make Miss Dearlove angry. This was a round-eyed look of panic and disbelief. They couldn't leave the cat behind – it would be too cruel. "The bombs. . ." she faltered.

"We are not taking a cat, certainly not a dirty stray like that. Why, even proper pets are. . ." She trailed off, shaking her head. "Get on, Emmie, we've a train to catch, halfway across the country! You're making us late. Now come along." Miss Dearlove went to seize Lucy from Emmie's arms, but Emmie screamed, and darted back, and Lucy hissed, not even sure who to be angry with. She fought and bit and scratched, and at last Emmie let go of her, with a despairing cry as the cat streaked away through the kitchen and the scullery, and out.

"At last! Now get out to the hallway and find your coat, we should have left by now. Mrs Evans, are you ready? The children are lining up," Miss Dearlove added to the cook, who was standing in the kitchen doorway watching,

But Emmie crouched to pick up the basket, gazing into it as if she almost couldn't believe it was empty.

"Put that down!" snapped Miss Dearlove, taking the handle.

Emmie jerked away, snatching it back. "No! I have to go and get her. We have to bring her with us!"

The matron grabbed the basket, and with the other hand she slapped Emmie across the cheek. Emmie dropped the cat basket, and leaned against the wall, tears seeping from the corners of her eyes. She wasn't crying because Miss Dearlove had hit her, even though it hurt, but because she'd realized that it was true – they meant it. They really were leaving Lucy behind.

"I couldn't help it," she heard Miss Dearlove murmur to the cook. "Dratted child, she does it on purpose. Bring her, will you, Mrs Evans? I need to go and lock up."

Emmie felt Mrs Evans's arm slide round her shoulders, and the cook's dry fingers stroked her scarlet cheek. She could hear the old woman tutting gently, but her voice seemed to come from a long way away.

"Come along, sweetheart. You come on now. Don't you worry about that little cat; she'll be next door, stealing a kipper for her breakfast, I expect. Time we were on our way."

Chapter Two

Emmie climbed wearily out of the train, her gas mask bumping against her hip, and the tiresome brown paper parcel clutched in her arms. They had been shut away in the stuffy compartments for hours, and even though they had changed trains at York, they hadn't had time for anything except a rush to the cloakrooms. Her legs felt stiff, almost like pins and needles, and her dress was clammy, sticking across her back.

The children and the three women stood rather helplessly gazing about the platform, until Miss Dearlove shook herself, and straightened her shoulders. "There'll be someone to meet us. Into line, come along." She crouched down and picked up Ruby, who was worn out and swaying on her feet, the bear dangling perilously from her hand.

The train suddenly spluttered, and creaked away with a great heave, leaving them alone at the tiny station. It was unbelievably quiet as the noise of the train faded, even quieter than the backstreet they were used to, where there was always a faint rumble of traffic. Here there was silence – except for a soft jingling of harness, from beyond the tiny station building. The late afternoon sun hung low, and there were bees murmuring over the grassy bank on the other side of the line.

A porter came hurrying up the platform with a trolley, from where he'd been unloading some wooden crates from the baggage car at the head of the train.

"Miss Dearlove? Th' car's outside for thee."

The children gaped at him, confused by his broad Yorkshire accent. Miss Dearlove smiled gratefully, and followed him through the little ticket office, and out to the yard beyond, where a strange mixture of vehicles stood waiting.

A man in a smart, dark uniform with a peaked cap nodded to Miss Dearlove, and then gently wrestled Ruby from her arms, propping her against his shoulder. Ruby was so exhausted, she simply eyed him for a moment, and then thumped her head into his jacket. The man looked at the children thoughtfully. "I reckon we can fit them all in th' cars, Miss. We brought the cart, for th' baggage." He inspected the children's parcels, then glanced back at the horse-drawn wagon, shook his head and smiled. "Bags won't fill it, will they?"

Miss Dearlove looked round at the weary line of children behind her, and sighed. "We couldn't bring very much with us – Miss Sowerby said in the telegram that bedding and such would be provided."

"Reckon there'll be enough." He snorted, and the man standing by the next car laughed. "I dunno. Sleeping nose to tail, tha'll be." The same strong accent made his words sound strange, but he was smiling.

The children stared at him, not understanding. Did he mean they'd have to share beds? The man beckoned to Emmie, and pointed into the second car, an enormous cream and black Austin. "Squash up in there, lass. Reckon there's room for seven or eight of you small ones in th' back."

Emmie clambered into the car, and the men lifted the others in after her, piling the little ones on the older children's laps. Emmie cringed as Tommy, one of the smallest boys, was pushed on to her knee – he was damp, and he smelled. She wasn't surprised – they'd been on the train all day, after all. She just tugged his coat further round his bottom, and wrinkled her nose.

Emmie peered out of the window round Tommy's knitted hood as they rolled away, the motion of the car smooth and quick, nothing like the jolting train. The station – Thwaite, it had said on the sign – seemed to be part of a tiny village. The car sped through, and it seemed hardly more than a church, and a few white-painted cottages. But every little house had a garden, bursting out over the fences. It was like nothing Emmie had ever seen before, and for a moment, a tiny, surprising, treacherous moment, she liked it.

The car wound along a narrow tree-lined road, gradually climbing, until the tall hedges opened out into a vast field of brownish-green. Emmie stared, and Tommy let out a squeak of surprise. It was like the park near the Home, but a thousand times over, a great, endless space of low bushes, grey and brown and faintly purple. "What is it?" Tommy whispered.

"I don't know," Emmie admitted. "A field? There's sheep, over there."

Tommy pressed his nose and his plump little hands against the window. "They're not fluffy. . ."

Emmie nodded. She'd never seen a real sheep, but there was a painting on the wall in the sitting room at the Home, and the sheep in it were whiter, and softer-looking. "Perhaps they're goats then. I don't know, do I?"

The colours deepened as the sun went down, and Emmie shivered. There was so much space. Sky everywhere. No streets. Even when they went to the park – which was only once a week or so – there were still buildings all around. This openness was frightening, it felt wrong, and it went on and on, without an end that she could see. Where were they going? What sort of place would be in the middle of the emptiness? Emmie gulped as they passed over a tiny stream rushing over rocks. Tommy laughed excitedly, pointing at the water, but Emmie flinched as the car bumped over the little humped bridge.

"Not far now," the man called back through the glass panel that divided the front and the back seats. "We're passing over the moor, and there's the drive up to th' house. See the trees?"

The dim golden light flickered and turned greenish as they rushed into a tunnel of great trees, looming over the road. Emmie leaned forward to see out at the front. "Here, look. This is where you're staying." The car broke out of the tree-lined tunnel, and pulled up in a stone courtyard at the front of a great grey house, shadowy and dim in the evening light.

The children bundled out, and stood huddled by the cars, even the smallest ones gazing silently at the house.

"It's a palace," muttered Arthur, and for once, Emmie didn't sneer at him. She thought maybe he was right. The grey stone walls surrounded the courtyard on three sides. The house wasn't very tall, and there were no turrets, or towers, but it looked *old*. The great blocks of dark stone were softened at the edges, and the windows were small and patched into tiny squares – and there were too many of them to count. The low evening sun glittered in the little panes, shining out under spidery trails of creeper.

The cars drew away, moving slowly off around one side, and leaving the children and the three women watching, as a huge wooden door opened in front of them. The light was bright, and for a moment the figure in the doorway showed only black, and Tommy stepped back into Emmie, clutching at her coat. But then the woman hurried down the steps, smiling, and holding out her hands.

"You're here, at last! Oh, you poor things, you must be exhausted. Welcome to Misselthwaite Manor."

Emmie lay in the high, carved wooden bed, watching the night light burning in its saucer of water, and peering at the room. The night light hardly gave enough light to see by, so it was half-looking, half-remembering, in a strange jumble of the day.

She was tired, but she'd slept in the train, and now she felt oddly restless. Ruby was fast asleep across the room, snuffling into her bear – and that was odd, for a start. Emmie was used to one huge room, with eight girls in it. Although this room would be about the size of the dormitory, if they took all the furniture out.

The candle flame jumped a little, and a creature glimmered in the light for a second: a horse with a thin, arched neck, and a jewelled bridle. The walls were covered in them, pictures made out of fabric, all castles and horses and dogs. Emmie had never seen anything like them before. She had never seen anything like this house. They had been hurried inside, the woman who had welcomed them explaining worriedly that they'd been told they mustn't show lights because of the new blackout regulations, but she'd thought they might trip over the furniture if she didn't turn the light on. A maid in uniform shut the door behind them with a slam, and the friendly woman shook Miss Dearlove's hand, and beamed at Miss Rose and Mrs Evans and the children.

"Mrs Craven?" Miss Dearlove asked, rather uncertainly.

"Oh! Yes, I'm so sorry. I'm Mrs Craven. I wish my husband could be here to welcome you too, but he went to London this morning. You probably passed his train going the other way." She gave a little laugh, but it sounded odd, as though she didn't think her joke was that funny. "He'd retired from the Navy when his father died, you see, but now that war is about to be declared, he's re-enlisting."

"Craven," Emmie whispered to Joey, who happened to be standing next to her. He was staring open-mouthed at a suit of armour that was standing up against the stone wall. If the hall hadn't been full of armour and weapons, it would have looked like a church, it was big enough. "The same name as the Home? Is that why we're here, you reckon?"

Joey dragged himself away from the armour, and the spears crossed over each other on the wall, and looked down at her in disgust. He was only a year older than she was, but he was a lot taller. "Course it is, stupid. This is the place, isn't it? Didn't you ever read that sign on the front of the Home? *Founded by Mr Archibald Craven of Misselthwaite Manor, in gratitude for the recovery of his son, Colin*? Misselthwaite, that's what she just said. Besides, I've seen her before." He nodded at the smiling woman, who was now talking to Miss Dearlove and Miss Rose, and pointing at the stairs. They were working out where to put all the children, Emmie thought. The man driving the car must have been teasing them, saying they'd have to sleep nose to tail. Surely a house like this would have enough beds?

"And so've you if you weren't so dim," Joey poked her in the ribs. "She comes to visit. She's one of the Board." The Board came twice a year, and their visits meant shoe-polishing, and even more frantic hair-brushing than usual, and Miss Rose panicking in case someone had made a mistake in their exercise books.

"You might have said," Emmie muttered, but Joey only rolled his eyes. She hadn't recognized Mrs Craven at all, but now she decided it might be because she had only seen her in a tailored suit and a smart hat, not an old tweed skirt and a cardigan. Miss Dearlove obviously hadn't known her straight off, either.

It was very strange, Emmie thought sleepily, to have no idea what would happen tomorrow. She was used to things being always the same. She lay staring towards the wall, hoping to see the horse leap again.

All they had been told was that they were to stay mostly in this part of the house – not that Emmie thought she would ever be able to find her way out of it anyway. After they'd had supper, they had been led back through the huge hall, up a polished wooden staircase, and in and out of corridors, down a few steps here and round a corner. The house was like a rabbit warren: all passages. Emmie had wondered wearily if they might lose Ruby, or one of the other little ones tagging along at the end of the line.

The red-cheeked woman who had shown them to their rooms had smiled at Emmie, and told her that the country air would be good for her, that she was far too thin.

"All bones," she added, patting her cheek. Emmie scowled. She knew she was too thin. Everyone always said so. She was even more thin because she'd been saving up her food for Lucy. Thinking of the little cat waiting for her on the fire escape only made Emmie scowl harder.

"Take that look off your face, Emmeline," Miss Dearlove snapped. "Say you're sorry to Miss Sowerby."

"Emmeline, there's a pretty name." Miss Sowerby seemed to be one of those people it was hard to offend. She just went on smiling, even when Emmie growled her apology. "You'll have this room, dear." She looked around it thoughtfully as she drew the curtains closed. "These curtains are good an' thick; we should be safe for this dratted blackout. Mr Craven went marching round the house last night, trying to see if there was a chink of light showing anywhere, but how do we keep a hundred rooms all covered up? Not that we use all the rooms, o' course. Most of the second floor is under dust sheets. Now, we've put another bed over here for one of th' smaller ones." She glanced down at Emmie again, still beaming. "We've had no little girls at Misselthwaite for many a year. Mr and Mrs Craven have two boys, I expect you'll meet Jack tomorrow. He must be about the same age as you."

Emmie nodded, and didn't say that she thought she had met him already. She wasn't sure, of course. But there had been a face peering down at them from a little flight of stairs, as they followed Miss Sowerby through yet another passage. A thin, angry face, with a scowl that Emmie didn't realize looked a great deal like her own.

The boy had seen Emmie watching, and stuck out his tongue. Everyone else had been so friendly, so sweetly concerned, that his furious face almost made Emmie feel better. She didn't care if the boy was rude – she could be just as rude back. She glanced round to check for Miss Dearlove, and put her own tongue out, waggling it at him gleefully.

Emmie smiled in the darkness, thinking of the surprise on the boy's face. Obviously, he hated them being here. Well, she hated being here too, and she didn't care who knew it.

Chapter Three

Emmie had hoped that with the upheaval of the move, lessons might be forgotten for a while, especially as not all the staff had come with them to Misselthwaite. Miss Rose and Miss Dearlove were managing on their own without the two younger nursery nurses, who had gone together to train in one of the great London hospitals. But Miss Rose had thought to send a trunk full of books ahead of them, and a room further along the passage had been set out as a schoolroom, with a strange assortment of heavy wooden tables, and unmatched chairs.

Emmie stared grimly down at her Historical Reader. Couldn't they have forgotten this one? She didn't mind the stories so much, but she knew them practically off by heart. Along with all the doodles and scratches and bent corners. She had drawn a moustache and a silly hat on Elizabeth I, and now every time she turned that page, it made her feel guilty.

She wasn't even sure that Miss Rose would notice if she slipped out. The teacher was too busy trying to cheer up Tommy, who'd wet his bed as he was too scared to get up in the dark, and was sure he was going to be sent back to the Home. He was too small to understand that there was no one to be sent back *to*.

Emmie propped her chin on her hand, and stared vaguely down at the page, letting the words sway between the lines and float into each other. The sun streamed through the deep-set windows, and made bars of light on the wooden table. She could see tiny specks of dust floating in the air. There were birds outside, she could hear them – different ones. Back in London it was mostly pigeons, and she had no idea what these were. Perhaps they could persuade Miss Rose to go on a nature walk, Emmie wondered sleepily. She had taken them to count the wildflowers in the park once.

Or they could explore the house – wouldn't

looking at all the paintings and the suits of armour tell them about history, anyway? It would be better than reading about King Alfred burning the cakes all over again. Emmie wasn't sure when Misselthwaite had been built, but it must be hundreds of years old. Miss Sowerby might tell them. Or even Mrs Craven. She'd asked Miss Dearlove to tell her anything she could do to help; Emmie had heard her.

"Have you finished, Emmie?"

Emmie's elbow slipped as she jumped, and she banged her wrist against the edge of the table. She didn't look up at Arthur and Joey on the other side of the table – she knew they'd be smirking. Being eleven instead of ten made them think they were so clever. "No, Miss," she muttered, cupping her hand over the bruise, and sucking her lips over her teeth. She'd hit it right on the bone.

"Stop dreaming and get on, then, please."

Emmie turned away from the sun patches on the wood, and gazed at the pages again, her eyes blurred and stinging.

"We can go out?" Emmie repeated, eyeing Miss Sowerby suspiciously. She was sure that this couldn't be right. "On our own? Anywhere in the gardens?"

"Anywhere." Miss Sowerby nodded, and then laughed at Arthur and Joey, who were suddenly gobbling down the last of their soup. "Use th' stairs at th' end of this passage, and they'll take you down to th' side door. These are your rooms, on this passage, you see. You're not to go to running about all over the house. But the gardens, you can explore. Mind you listen out for th' gardeners – if they tell thee to keep off, you keep off."

"And be back by two," Miss Dearlove added. "For afternoon lessons." She sounded suddenly anxious, as though she thought she might lose them. "We're trusting you three older ones; the littler children will stay closer to the house, with Miss Rose and me."

"How are we to know when it's two o'clock?" Joey asked suddenly, and Arthur elbowed him in the side. Emmie scowled. None of them had wristwatches, of course. She looked crossly at Miss Rose and Miss Dearlove. Now they wouldn't be allowed to go.

"There's a clock in the little tower over the courtyard," Miss Sowerby told them calmly. "Go by that. You'll hear it chime the hours, and the quarters." She gave Arthur a sharp glance. "Don't you ask me where th' courtyard be, boy. Use some gumption, go an' find it!"

Arthur and Joey raced away. Emmie could hear them clattering down the wooden staircase. She wanted to bolt the rest of her food and run after them, but she held herself back, spooning up the last of the soup. She was almost sure that she would be stopped, somehow. If she rushed, and looked excited, someone was sure to call her and make her stay in after all. Even as she walked down the stairs, and heaved at the heavy door, she was still waiting for Miss Dearlove to yank her back.

But no one did. Emmie stood hesitating in the doorway, staring out at the garden. It seemed strange for the sun to be so bright. With war being declared, and all the whispers about London being bombed, everything had felt grey – even the view from the train windows. The moor had been tinted grey and violet in the evening sun, faded with shadows, and her misery over leaving Lucy.

Now she stood blinking at the whiteness of the gravel walk that led between the clipped yew trees. The yews were almost black in the sunlight, and the creeper growing up the stone wall of the old house blazed a wild green. Emmie put out her hand, and rubbed one of the leaves, running it through her shaking fingers. She'd thought it would be rough, but instead it felt soft, almost soapy.

This was like another world, fresh, and brilliantly alive – and then she remembered that it was hers only for an hour.

Emmie pulled the door shut behind her with a bang. She could hear the boys, shouting and whooping somewhere in the distance, and she deliberately turned away from the noise. She wanted to explore by herself. The path seemed made to run down, leading to a thick, dark hedge, trimmed into an archway. Beyond, Emmie could see more of the tempting green. She slipped through, catching her breath as the closed walk opened up into a stretch of perfect lawn. The grass looked like a carpet, clipped short, and she crouched down, running her hands over it and smiling to herself.

Then she turned, glancing back at the house. Could anyone see her? She could just imagine Miss Dearlove, rolling her eyes at that Emmie, stroking the grass... But the small diamond-paned windows glittered in the sun, and she couldn't see anyone looking out. Wasn't she away from their part of the house now, anyway? She frowned – the place was so big, it was hard to tell. But the gardens were huge too – she could see that now. There were walls and hedges and terraces, so the great space was divided up, almost like rooms in a house. But on this higher bit of ground, she could see how far they spread out – for miles, it looked like. Even if someone did glance out of a window, Emmie was almost sure they wouldn't see her. She felt deliciously small, and secret. There was no one in sight, no one at all.

She stood up, and stretched out her arms, feeling the sun on her hands and wrists – her cardigan was on the small side, and the sleeves rode up. She went a few steps further, enough to look down the slope at the end of the lawn. There were stone steps set into the side of the bank, a crumbly grey stone that was golden in the sun. They led down to a pool, darkly gleaming, and scattered with white, waxen-looking flowers.

Emmie hurried down the steps to crouch at the edge of the water. There were little golden fish hovering below the surface, and as her shadow fell across the pond, they swam lazily towards her. Perhaps they hoped she'd come to feed them, Emmie thought, and she sat down heavily on the stone paving, suddenly reminded of Lucy. How long had Lucy waited on the fire escape, the day before?

Had she found enough to eat, scavenging from someone else?

Emmie stared into the water, wishing that there was a little black cat sitting here too, watching those fish. Or stretched out basking on the sun-warmed stone. Her fingers twitched, wanting dark fur to stroke.

She sprang up angrily, scattering the golden fish, and stalked away past the pool, and the glittering fountain. The sun and the scents of the flowers and the spicy smell of the yew hedges had made her forget how lost she felt. But she didn't belong here. She didn't belong *anywhere*. Emmie sped up, running along the edge of the pool. She swiped blindly at the flowers in the long bed down the side of the water garden, raising a gust of sharp lemon scent, and a hum of bees. The garden was bordered with another dark hedge, and she darted through an archway at the corner, fists clenched, furious with the perfection, the trimmed prettiness of it all. She would rather be hiding away from everyone else on a broken old iron fire escape. She didn't care how beautiful the place was.

Someone laughed, and Emmie heard running footsteps close by. She turned away sharply, not wanting the boys to find her. She was on a brick path now, less grand than the stone terraces around the fountain. One side was bordered by the hedge, and the other by a long brick wall, trailing gleaming curtains of leaves. The creeper was flowering in clouds of tufted yellow balls, and bees droned in and out of it. Emmie had no idea what the dark leaves were, but she liked the gleam of them, and she slowed a little to watch the bees, sharply buzzing little ones, and great fat sleepy furry things that lurched from flower to flower.

She was about to hurry on, realizing that the boys must have been heading back to the house, when a sharp trilling song sounded above her head, and she stepped back, staring up in surprise. At first Emmie thought Arthur or Joey had somehow climbed on top of the wall, but there was no one there – only a tiny red-breasted bird, peering curiously at her out of the ivy.

"A robin!" Emmie stared at him. She didn't think she'd ever seen one for real before. She had seen Christmas cards, and Miss Rose had shown them how to draw a Christmas robin, but for some reason Emmie had assumed that robins were part of the same storybook Christmas as parties and crackers and stockings and camels.

The little bird leaned further out to look at her, with his head on one side. He was brownish, and soft-looking, and the breeze ruffled the red fluff of his breast-feathers. He trilled again, staring at her with bright black bead eyes.

"You know I'm new," Emmie whispered. "New and different. There hasn't been a little girl here for years and years, Miss Sowerby said." She took a step closer, and watched as the robin's beak shimmered and trembled with the bright notes. It was magical. Then he stopped, and looked at her sideways, proud and shy at the same time, and Emmie screwed up her face and whistled back to him.

"I have to go," she murmured. "They said we had to be on time for lessons, and I might be late already. It isn't that I want to go," she assured him, and then stopped herself. What was she talking to a bird for? But his eyes were so bright, and knowing. She was almost sure he understood. He fluttered up a few branches, perched on top of the wall, and then darted away with a flick of his tail.

Emmie turned and ran, back along the path, through the hedge and along the terrace past the fountain, racing back up the stairs to fling herself pink-cheeked and breathless into the schoolroom.

"Goodness!" Miss Rose stared at her, and Arthur and Joey smirked angelically.

"I got lost," Emmie said quickly. "I couldn't find the right door."

The boy standing next to Miss Rose gave a tiny snort, and Miss Rose seemed to remember that he was there. "Yes. Jack, this is Emmie – she's ten, like you."

Emmie suppressed a sigh. She had always hated it that there was no one her own age at the Craven Home, but she wasn't going to be friendly with this boy – the boy who'd been making faces round the banisters – just because he was ten. Especially not if everybody wanted her to...

"Emmie, this is Jack – Mrs Craven's son. He was at boarding school, but he's had measles, so he's staying at home for now."

"I'm going back," the boy snapped. "Any day."

"Of course." Miss Rose smiled. "But for the moment, Jack will be doing some lessons with us."

The boy rolled his eyes, and Joey, Arthur and Emmie watched him suspiciously – united for once in their dislike of this stranger. A stranger who actually belonged in this house.

"Boarding school?" Arthur muttered to Joey, as

Jack slid into a seat across the table. "This lot are weird."

Jack glared at Arthur, but he didn't say anything. He was silent for the whole morning, working swiftly through the maths questions that Miss Rose set for them, and shoving them in front of her when she came back from the table where the smaller ones were copying their letters. Miss Rose looked taken aback, as if she hadn't expected him to polish the work off so quickly. Emmie and the other boys stared at him in disgust. Posh *and* clever, then.

Jack looked down his nose, and as soon as Miss Rose announced, in a relieved voice, that it was half-past three, he slipped out of his seat and disappeared.

"Stuck-up little so-and-so," Joey growled under his breath, and Emmie nodded, which surprised them both.

Chapter Four

There had been no church that morning – only hymns, and Miss Dearlove reading from the book of Bible stories, and looking twitchily at the little clock on the mantelpiece and falling over her words. Then at eleven they had trooped downstairs to the servants' hall, squeezing in among the maids and gardeners. The cook and Mrs Evans had made tea, but hardly anyone was drinking it. Instead they perched uncomfortably on the chairs gathered round the polished wooden radio. The whole house must be there, Emmie thought, trying to count the servants without letting anyone see that she was staring. Miss Dearlove had explained to them at breakfast that the prime minister was going to speak; it was very important. The matron hadn't said quite how, but she was jumpy and nervous, and even friendly Miss Sowerby looked anxious.

As the words, "This is London..." echoed through the sunny room, Emmie saw that Mrs Craven and Jack had slipped in too, and one of the gardeners had swiftly given up his chair. Mrs Craven smiled at the boy, and patted his arm. Jack leaned against her shoulder, darting cold glances at the other children. Arthur and Joey were rolling a marble along the crack between the flagstones, and Tommy was whining to Miss Rose that he was hungry.

But as the broadcast went on, even the smallest ones grew silent, frozen by the dreadful sense of sadness and frustration in the voice coming from the radio cabinet. Miss Dearlove was clutching Ruby on her lap, and Emmie saw her rest her face in Ruby's hair just for a moment. She was so shocked by Miss Dearlove's frightened eyes that it took her several seconds to understand what Mr Chamberlain had said.

And that consequently this country is at war with Germany.

It was almost an anti-climax – she *knew* that. That was why they had been dragged out of London, wasn't it? Had they all been hoping that it wouldn't happen after all? Emmie glanced around under her eyelashes at the men and women in the room. Their fear felt so real that she was almost sure she could touch it. She jumped a little as the miserable voice died away, and a great pealing of bells rang out – and all the frozen statues in the room shifted, and gasped, and the maids turned to hug each other. Several of them were crying.

"Ssshhh, listen." Miss Sowerby nodded towards the radio again – a man was now solemnly repeating instructions about air-raid sirens, and shelters. "The cellar. We'll have to use the cellar for an air-raid shelter. It's the safest place." Miss Sowerby looked over at Mrs Craven, who nodded, and gave a little cough.

"We'll start this afternoon. I shouldn't think they'd come here, but in case…"

"We could build some bunks, ma'am," one of the gardeners suggested. "Better get some hurricane lanterns down there."

And then everyone stumbled to their feet, hauling up the confused children to stand for *God Save the King*. No one sang, only listened, heads bowed. Emmie wondered if the king was still in London, and the little princesses, or had they been evacuated too?

She was probably supposed to be in the cellars now, but she'd slipped out to the gardens again instead. Miss Dearlove had said that after lunch they could all help to clean and dust. But even with lanterns, Emmie couldn't bear to be down there in the dark and shadows. They'd slept two nights at Misselthwaite Manor now, and she'd seen how strange and dark it was, even above ground. The little night light on her bedside table had seemed nothing against the weight of the darkness outside the windows. The Yorkshire nights were black in a way that Emmie was sure London never could be, and the stars looked cold. But London's street lights had been turned out now. Miss Dearlove had explained that to them, when Ruby complained she hated the dark. This was war. All the country was night-black, to give the bombers nothing to see. The thought made Emmie shiver, and run to the light and the warmth of the gardens.

She ran her fingers along the brick wall that edged the path, and then rubbed them together, brushing away the powdery redness. This path ran all along the side of the kitchen gardens and the orchard,

Emmie knew now. She still hadn't explored all of the gardens, not even half of them, probably. But the kitchen gardens were interesting – there were plants under strange glass bells, and tall wooden towers with what seemed to be beans hanging off them. They looked like good places to hide and spy and nose, and Emmie had been down this path a few times now.

The wall was soft and worn, with fat cushions of faded velvet moss between the bricks. Towards the far end of the path, the wall was covered in a thick curtain of those glossy dark leaves. The door to the kitchen garden was open, and Emmie peered round it curiously. She didn't think anyone would be here – she wouldn't have to skirt around the edges of the garden, trying not to be seen.

All the gardeners had been in the servants' hall – even those who were married, and would spend Sundays at their own cottages, had come in to listen to the prime minister's message. The cellars would be for them and their families too, if there should be an air raid. Everyone was down there now, planning how to furnish them, and strengthen the roof beams, and wondering whether the coal chute could be turned into some sort of emergency door in case the house were to collapse on top of them. When the butler had said that, everyone else had turned to stare at him in horror, and he'd reddened and looked apologetically at Emmie and the other children. But then he shrugged. It happened – he had fought on the Somme, he had seen the craters. The bombs they were talking of these days... Of course, there was no airfield nearby – yet – and they were a long way away from York, or any other town, but they were not far from the coast. And everyone nodded, and swallowed, and tried not to think of the weight of stone above their heads.

No one had told them they were not to explore these working gardens, but Emmie had only peered round the doors until now, as there had always been gardeners in there working. They were friendly – one of them had smiled at her and asked her how she was settling in. She'd just given him her stare. Emmie had been avoiding company, unlike Arthur and Joey, who'd taken less than a day to discover that there were apples and plums in the orchard, and gardeners who might look the other way while they climbed the trees, particularly if they'd help with the weeding or pick stones in return.

Now the gardens were deserted, sun-warmed and

silent. She could wander around the little paths, and peer at the vegetables – most of which she didn't recognize, since she'd only ever seen them boiled to within an inch of their lives. Perhaps she would see the robin again, she thought, glancing around hopefully. Birds ate vegetables, didn't they? He had been on the creeper-covered part of the wall when she saw him before, very close to here.

Padding quietly along, Emmie walked round a thicket of beans, the last few pods still dangling from their frame, and nearly tripped over a man tying in the stems. She skipped back, gasping, and then took another hurried step back when he looked up at her.

"Who are you?"

Emmie was silent for a moment. It wasn't the Yorkshire accent that made him hard to understand. The tight skin of the scars that covered one side of his face had pulled his mouth sideways, and slurred his voice. She swallowed. "I'm allowed to be here."

"Never said tha' weren't."

"Why aren't you with the others? Building bunks, and … and things." Emmie shrugged vaguely.

"Bunks?" He frowned at her.

"They're making the cellars into an air-raid shelter. Because now we're at war." It was the first time she had said it – somehow she felt it ought to have been more dramatic.

"Are we?" he muttered. "That why th'art here, then? One of those evacuee children Mrs Craven mentioned?"

"Yes. Didn't you go and listen to the radio this morning? I thought everybody did."

"Happen everybody doesn't want t'know."

Cautiously, Emmie moved a step closer to him. She wanted to ask what had happened to his face, but she couldn't think of a way to say it politely. She suspected he'd been injured in the Great War – like the lame man who came to the Home every few weeks to sharpen knives. She was just trying to frame the words, when a little streak of red-and-brown fluttered past, and landed between her and the man, glancing between them curiously.

"Oh, the robin!" Emmie crouched down to look at him closer.

"Tha' knows him, then?" The man looked at her thoughtfully.

"I saw him yesterday. He was sitting in all those green leaves on the wall."

"Ivy, that is."

"Ivy," Emmie murmured, not really paying

attention. She was trying to chirrup at the robin, who was looking at her with his head on one side, quite confused.

"I don't think I'm making the right noises. . ."

"Nor do I."

"Well, there's no need to be rude." Emmie glared at him, and then the robin shot up into the air and landed on the man's shoulder, its little scaly claws digging into his velveteen waistcoat.

"Tha'll fright him, wi' that sharp voice," the man said, his own voice very gentle – soft under the strange slurring.

"Sorry. . ." Emmie dropped her voice to a whisper. "Why does he sit on you? Does he like you?"

"Known him from the egg, I suppose. He hatched out here, in this garden – one close by, at any rate. And I move slow." His face twisted a little, and the scars crinkled. Emmie tried not to grimace, but her eyes flickered, and her mouth twisted too, in a moment of disgust.

"Even slower now," he added, in a growl under his breath. And suddenly he heaved himself up, so that the robin sprang away from his shoulder, spreading out his wings to catch the air, like little brown fans. The man grabbed at a wooden crutch that had been lain down beside him – Emmie had thought the crutch was some sort of garden tool, but now as he stomped down the path leaning on it, she saw that part of his leg was made of metal. The robin swooped around his head, chittering fiercely as the gardener made for the door at the other end of the garden, and then it fluttered away over the wall.

Emmie stared after them, wishing she hadn't made a face – she hadn't meant to. She'd liked the man, even if he had been as grumpy as she was. She could see that she'd made him angry – or sad. And she longed for the robin to land on her shoulder too.

She trailed around the vegetable beds for a little longer, hoping at least to see the robin again, but he had disappeared. There were only a couple of blackbirds, pecking hopefully at a fruit net, and they swooped away almost as soon as she had seen them.

"I suppose I ought to go back," Emmie murmured, trying to speak softly, like the gardener had said. If she stayed out long enough to make them worry, Miss Dearlove might keep her indoors the next day. If she was lucky, everyone had been too busy and anxious to notice she wasn't there. She ran along the path to the shrubbery, laughing a little as she felt the wind blowing her hair back.

Then she stopped, pressing herself back against the scratchy yew hedge, and straightening her face to a proper, wartime seriousness. Mrs Craven was walking towards her.

Emmie ducked her head politely, hoping that the lady would just walk past, but she didn't. She stopped and leaned down to talk.

"Are you having fun out here?"

"I didn't mean to," Emmie said swiftly.

"Oh, I wasn't saying you shouldn't. It's lovely to see you running about." She swallowed. "I hope all that doesn't change."

Emmie looked up cautiously, not sure if this was meant for her to hear. Mrs Craven sounded more as if she were talking to herself.

"Were you exploring the gardens?"

"Yes. I was looking at the vegetables. I met a gardener," Emmie added. "He made a robin sit on his shoulder."

"Oh! That would be Mr Sowerby. He can charm the birds out of the trees – when he tries." She looked down at Emmie in surprise. "Did he speak to you?"

"He told me my voice was too sharp," Emmie said, frowning. "And that he knew the robin when he was an egg. Mr Sowerby like Miss Sowerby in the house?"

"Yes, her brother." Mrs Craven put her hand on Emmie's shoulder. "He doesn't talk to people much these days – don't be upset if he should bark at you, will you?"

"Did he hurt his leg in the war?"

"At the very end of the war." Mrs Craven sighed. "It's never healed properly since. It hurts him. And he remembers things." She tried to smile at Emmie. "I know it's a long time ago. Long before you were born, or my Jack, or even David. But it doesn't feel all that long, sometimes."

Emmie nodded. Miss Dearlove probably wouldn't want her talking to Mrs Craven at all, but she wanted to know – now was her chance to know more than Joey, and Arthur. "David?" she asked politely. "Is that another of your children? I only knew there was Jack."

Mrs Craven glanced down again, blinking, almost as if she'd forgotten that Emmie was there. "Yes. Of course, you've not met him. My older son, he's gone to join the RAF." She pressed her hand against her mouth for a moment, and murmured something to Emmie about enjoying the day. Then she hurried away down the path and whisked round the hedge, but Emmie could see that she was still standing there. She was hiding – like Emmie did when she was trying not to cry.

Shaken, Emmie crept away, trying not to let the gravel scrunch under her shoes, and slipped in through the side door to find the others. Perhaps there were worse things than being afraid of the heavy dark on the moor.

Emmie kicked at Ruby's bear, which was lying on the floor by her little cot bed. She could hear Ruby and the others laughing and squealing as they chased each other across the lawn below the window.

Of course Miss Dearlove *had* noticed that Emmie wasn't helping in the cellars the day before – Miss Rose had even gone to look for her, so they said, when she turned up *looking like butter wouldn't melt, after we'd been worrying ourselves sick over you all afternoon*. Emmie thought that they looked downright cross rather than worried, but for once she'd had the sense not to say so.

After breakfast Miss Dearlove had confined her to her room, and given her dusters, and some wax polish, and told her to tidy it up. Emmie had rubbed a little of the polish into the dark wood table by her bed, so that the room smelled pleasantly of lavender and they couldn't say she hadn't tried – and then gone back to looking out of the window. Even the misty purplish slopes of the moor looked welcoming, now that she was shut up. But listening to the others playing only made her feel crosser, when she had to stay indoors for a whole day. Miss Dearlove had said she would let Emmie out for lessons, but that wasn't much better than being stuck in her bedroom, except that it gave her a chance to scowl at Jack across the table.

Emmie sighed, and thumped down on Ruby's bed, which creaked painfully, and sagged a bit. Then she picked up the bear, and stroked him a little to say sorry, and sat him up against the pillow.

What was she going to *do*? Even though Miss Rose's boring lessons seemed to go on for hours, they actually didn't take up that much of the day. Since the two nurses who'd cared for the younger children back at the Home hadn't come with them, it meant Miss Rose was too busy looking after the little ones to teach anyone very much. So Emmie could be stuck in this room for hours. She couldn't even read, since the books were all in the schoolroom. There had to be something in here to do, surely.

Emmie got up, and stood in the middle of the room, watching the tiny specks of dust falling in the sunlight from the window. She supposed she could actually dust and polish the furniture, like she'd been told... It would pass the time, anyway. Grumpily, she went to fetch the jar of polish from the little bedside table, and leaned over to pick up the rags, which had slipped down underneath it. Crouched down like that, she noticed for the first time that the table had a drawer. She wasn't really expecting to find anything interesting in there – but there might perhaps be an old pack of cards, so she could play patience.

She tugged at the drawer – it stuck, as though no one had tried to open it for years, and then flew open sharply, so that the old notebooks inside slid about.

Emmie sighed. The books didn't look very exciting. There were three of them, all with faded cloth covers. They looked like the book Miss Dearlove made the laundry lists in.

She pulled one out, and flicked through it – it was full of tiny, closely written notes, but not a laundry list. It was more like a story. And even though the writing was old-fashioned and scratchy and grown-up-looking, the spelling was quite bad. Bad enough to make Emmie snigger. It was then she realised that the books were diaries – a child's diaries, she was almost sure. She had never heard of anyone writing a diary before, but there were dates written here and there. It was the story of someone's life. Suddenly interested, she scrabbled in the drawer and got out all three books, searching through them to find the earliest dates.

The most faded book of the three was red, its cloth worn to pink in patches, and the spine a little split. Emmie smiled to herself when she saw the date written on the opening page – January 1910. This was the first.

There was something written in faint brown ink on the inside of the cover, and she picked it up and took it over to the light of the window to read.

Mary Lennox
Misselthwaite Manor
This is not my book, but no one wants it, so I am making it my diary. No one will care.

Mary Lennox... Emmie rolled the name around on her tongue. She liked it. So this was a girl's diary. Someone around her own age? That angry, scrawled line made her think so.

Emmie forgot about polishing entirely, and put the later diaries back into the drawer. Then she lay down on top of her bed, with the limp notebook propped against the pillow. One of the pages was coming loose from the stitching, and as she slid it back in, a few words seemed to leap at her.

soft scarlet feathers, and thin, spindly little legs ... I wish he would make friends with me ... I haven't a friend of my own...

Emmie stared at the page, swallowing hard. She felt as though there was something hard lodged in her throat. This Mary had felt just the same way she had – and she had seen a robin in the garden too. Perhaps her robin was the great-great-great-grandfather of Emmie's.

But if she lived here, and this great, huge house was really her home, why *didn't* Miss Mary have any friends? She must have been so rich, Emmie thought. She must have had everything she ever wanted. Emmie turned back through the pages to the beginning of the diary, frowning to herself.

I do not like this place, and I do not want to stay here. But I have nowhere else to go.

Even in the faded ink the words seemed to shimmer on the page, and Emmie stroked her fingers across them. Someone else had felt so much like she did.

There was a noise of running feet in the passageway outside, and Emmie slapped the book shut and stuffed it back into the drawer. Then she snatched up the cloth, and began to rub it over the carved post at the corner of her bed, with a cross, pinched expression on her face – just as they expected to see her.

Miss Rose opened the door and sighed, very faintly. "Come on, Emmie. Lessons."

Emmie stalked after her to the schoolroom, but her scowl was only to keep up appearances. If those notebooks were in her room, then they were hers, weren't they? No one could mind her reading them. Not that she was going to ask anyway. She was almost sure that Miss Mary, whoever she was, wouldn't mind.

"Stop daydreaming, Emmie!" Miss Rose tapped her nails on the table in front of Emmie's book, and Emmie blinked at her. She had been thinking about the robin, the rich orange-red of his feathers, and the way he'd looked at her with his head sideways, as though he thought she was interesting. Hardly anybody thought she was interesting, ever. She was just a nuisance, except to Lucy. It was stupid for a bird to make her remember a cat, but he did. He'd looked at her the same way – curious, a little bit suspicious. Emmie had tamed Lucy – perhaps she could tame the robin too?

"Dolly Daydream!" Joey whispered, smirking. "What were you thinking about, then?"

Emmie rolled her eyes at him. As if she'd tell.

"She's dreaming about that stupid cat again." Arthur poked her arm with his pencil. "Weren't you? See, she was, she's gone red." He was bored, and teasing Emmie was good value, if he could make her lose her temper.

"Wasn't. . ." Emmie muttered, hating the way she blushed so easily. Why shouldn't she think about Lucy? "And what if I was, anyway?"

"What cat?" Jack asked, and they all stared at him. He didn't speak in their lessons, unless Miss Rose asked him a direct question. For the last two days he had trudged into the schoolroom with a haughty look on his face, and slid out again as soon as he could. He'd never spoken to any of them before.

"She had a cat, back in London," Arthur said, after a moment of silence. "Skinny black thing, a stray. Fed it half your food, didn't you, Emmie? That's why she's so skinny too."

"And then she made an almighty fuss when Miss Dearlove wouldn't let her bring it with us," Joey added. "She cried."

Arthur sniggered. "She's going to cry again, look."

Emmie dug her fingers into her palms hard, so the nails left purple half-moons in the skin. "I'm not." She swallowed the tears back with a huge effort, and glared, not at Joey and Arthur, but at Jack. This was his fault. He'd asked. They might have let her alone if he hadn't asked.

He gazed back at her, his grey eyes hard, like shining stones. "So you left your cat behind?"

Emmie didn't answer him. She didn't trust him.

"You know what's happening to cats and dogs in London, don't you?"

Arthur leaned further over the table, glancing back towards Miss Rose, who was busy counting wooden bricks with the smaller ones. "What? There hasn't been bombs yet, we'd have heard about it."

"Destroyed. All of them." Jack was still staring at Emmie. "*Killed*. Because there isn't going to be enough food to feed them. And because they'll be so scared of the bombs they'll go mad. There was a leaflet sent out about it back in the summer, telling people it was the best thing to do. A leaflet from the government, like all those leaflets about shelters, and gas masks. Thousands of cats and dogs are getting put down. They take them to the vets, and the vets—"

"That isn't true," Emmie burst out. "You're just saying it because … because you hate us."

Jack shrugged. "I do hate you. But it's still true. It made my mother cry, when she read about it in the newspaper. Some duchess is trying to get people to send them all to her country house, but it's too late now." He smiled, triumphantly, and Emmie could only shake her head. It was horrible; it couldn't be true. But the duchess made it all sound real. How could he make that up?

"Lucy wasn't a proper pet…" she whispered. "No

one would take her to the vets."

He shrugged. "I bet they're catching strays too."

"Why would they?" Joey broke in suddenly. "Stop sniffing, Emmie. He's just saying it because he wants to see you cry."

Emmie looked round at Joey, her eyes hot and blurred with tears. Was he actually sticking up for her?

"No one could catch that skinny thing except for you anyway. She'll be all right. Bet she can run faster than a bomb."

Arthur nodded, and then sniggered. "And she'll be all right in the blackout, won't she? She'll fit right in."

Emmie snorted tearily. It was an odd feeling, to have them on her side for once.

"Think what you like. No skin off my nose." Jack glanced up at them, and his eyes glittered. He dropped his voice. "Anyway, she knows I'm right."

Mary Lennox
Misselthwaite Manor
14th January 1910

I have been out into the gardens, because there is nothing else for me to do. It is much colder here, and everything is grey, even the sky. There is a fountain, but it hasn't any water in it, just a lot of dead leaves.

There was a bird sitting in one of the trees. I asked an old man who is one of the gardeners, and he told me that the bird is a robin. He chirped at me – it almost felt like he was talking to me. He had a brown body, and a front covered in soft scarlet feathers, and thin spindly little legs. He isn't like any bird I've seen in India. When I saw him first he was sitting in the very highest branch of a tree over a wall. I tried to follow him, but there was no door to the garden full of trees. I think that the robin was in the garden that has been locked up for years and years.

Martha, the maid, told me about this locked garden, and one of the gardeners too. I tried to ask him where the door was, but he was cross and said I was meddlesome.

I want to see the garden, but it doesn't have a door, or not that I can find, and I walked all the way round. There are two kitchen gardens and then the orchard, but there is another garden beyond that, with no way to get inside it at all.

The robin was in the locked garden, I'm almost sure he was. I am going to find the door, or perhaps I shall climb over the wall. Then I could see the robin again. He sang so loudly, and he liked me, I think. I wish he would make friends with me.

I don't think I have ever had a friend, and I should like one.

Chapter Five

Emmie wriggled herself further under the quilt, fighting to stay asleep. She was warm, and if she woke up properly she would know how dark it was. The wind was screaming around the house, blowing down off the great purple slope of the moor. It howled in the chimney like a wild beast, and Emmie didn't want to wake up and have to think about it. She pulled the quilt right over her head, and that warm, breathless darkness felt safe. But it was too hot and stuffy to stay huddled underneath for long. She burrowed out like a mouse, and lay twitching and listening to the wind, and Ruby's thin little snore. The diary slithered slowly down the heaped patchwork quilt, and thumped on to the floor, but Emmie felt too edgy to reach down and pick it up.

The wild beast noises were dying down now, but they were still eerie. Just strange little hiccupping cries – what made the wind do that? Perhaps it was an owl? Perhaps there was an owl sitting on the windowsill and wailing. Arthur had seen one, swooping down low over the courtyard – or so he had said.

Emmie shivered, even though the room was so warm, waiting to hear the *tap-tap-tap* of a beak. She was properly awake now, it was no good pretending she wasn't. She sat up, huddling her arms around her knees, and listening. However many times she told herself the noise was only the wind, it did sound as though something was trying to force its way in. She jumped as the windows rattled again, and gasped for breath.

The wind dropped to a still calm that was just as frightening – the empty space where the sound had been echoed around her. Emmie buried her face in the quilt over her knees and waited for the wind to roar and slam itself against the walls again.

But it didn't. Instead a thin, sobbing wail echoed down the passageway, so quiet and sad that it made Emmie gasp, and whimper herself.

That was not the wind. She'd heard it earlier too, she realized, but she had thought the stifled gasps were part of the storm battling down from the moor. Now she was almost sure the noise wasn't an owl either. It was somebody else, crying.

She peered over at Ruby – no, she was definitely fast asleep. Miss Rose and Miss Dearlove slept next door to the rooms with the smaller children in, so if it was one of them crying, surely they'd have got up to see what was the matter? But she couldn't hear footsteps, or anyone talking. Just the sobs, worn out and miserable, as though whoever was making them didn't expect anyone to come. They were only crying because they couldn't not.

Emmie shuddered. What if only she could hear the noise, because it was a ghost crying in the dark? The house was old and full of history enough to be haunted, after all. Then she wrinkled her nose thoughtfully. If there was even a rumour of a ghost at Misselthwaite, that stuck-up Jack would have told her and Arthur and Joey. He would have done his best to scare them silly. In fact, she was quite surprised that he hadn't invented a ghost, and dressed up in a sheet to try and catch them out.

But still – in the dark, it was hard not to believe in ghosts. . .

Another weary cry whispered into the room, and Emmie got out of bed. She wasn't sure if she was going to see what was the matter, or if she was going to tell whoever it was to shut up. She just couldn't listen to that sad noise any more.

The Manor had electric light in most of the rooms, but because there were so many windows, and the staff hadn't been able to fit proper blackout curtains over all of them, the children had been given candlesticks to carry if they needed to visit the lavatory at the end of the passage. Emmie lit her candle from the night-light flame and marched out into the passageway, clicking the door shut gently behind her. The passage looked darker even than her bedroom, and the blackness seemed to rush in on the small flame of her candle, as if it would like to swallow it up. Huge grey shadow-monsters loomed up the walls as Emmie began to walk towards the noise. It didn't help to know that they were only her own shadow, thrown by the darting candle flame. What if the candle blew out? Then the shadows might leap on her.

Emmie knew that was stupid, but she couldn't

help believing it anyway, just a little. Breathing fast, she cupped her hand painfully close around the flame, and hurried down the passage, trying to work out which door the crying was coming from.

She got all the way to the little staircase where Jack had hidden on the first night – was that really only three nights ago? But then the noise seemed hard to pin down – as though it was echoing back from somewhere else. Perhaps that was only the wind... Emmie stood hesitating at the bottom of the steps, wondering whether to go up. But the wind had died down again, and the night was peaceful. Had she imagined it then?

The candle flame skittered sideways in a sudden draught, and Emmie gasped as the shadows flung themselves in great tearing leaps around the panelled staircase. Perhaps the crying had stopped because the ghost was just behind her now, instead. It had tempted her in...

She shut her eyes tight, wishing for Lucy, Miss Rose, even Miss Dearlove, anyone. But there was only the faint creak of the floorboards, her own weight shifting. She was all alone, and the night was still. Perhaps no one had been crying after all.

26th January 1910

I am sure it was magic.

The robin showed me the key, buried in the hole – but something made him look for worms just there, just then. I might not have picked it up – it looked so worn and rusted and dirty. But I had to, because I knew it was the key to the garden that had been locked for ten years. I still couldn't find the door, but the key in my pocket made me think that I would, one day.

It was when I went out to skip with the rope that Martha's mother sent me. I had never seen a skipping rope, but Martha showed me – she can skip to a hundred. I can't skip to any more than thirty before I get tired, but I will get better. I skipped almost all the way down the walk by the locked garden, and the robin came to watch me.

He sat on the top of the wall and sang to make me look at him, and it was magic, because it meant I was watching when the wind blew through the ivy. He made me look, and I saw the brown metal of the door handle, just for a second. The door was painted green like all the others, but so faded and worn and covered in ivy that I never knew it was there. The ivy hangs down like a thick curtain, and I crept underneath it, and opened the door with the key.

It was so still. So quiet – but then no one has spoken inside it for ten years. Only the birds have been there. Everything was covered in great grey trails of roses; they've climbed and clambered over the trees and the benches and the statues and they've even gone snaking out over the grass in some places. They've grown everywhere, but I think they're dead – they look so dry and grey. I wish they weren't. I wish I'd seen the garden how it was ten years ago, with all the roses flowering. But then it wouldn't have been so quiet and secret and mine. I can play my own stories there, and no one will watch me, or laugh. I have been digging around the bulbs, and there are hundreds, maybe even thousands of them, all sending up little green points. I pulled the grass away to help them breathe. I don't know what to do to help the roses though. I don't know how to make them grow.

I asked the gardener about roses, but he snarled at me again – he is the most bad-tempered person I have ever met. He might even be sulkier than me. The housekeeper said I was nasty-tempered, I heard her, and Martha is always saying how strange I am. But in my Secret Garden, I am only me, and no one minds.

And I have the key – the only key! I am keeping it in the drawer where I hide this diary, to make sure no one sees.

Emmie gripped the pages tighter, breathing fast, her heart jumping. Mary had a place all of her own – a secret, like Lucy had been Emmie's secret. And now the diaries were in Emmie's drawer. In *her* bedside table. So maybe the key...

She sat up in bed, the diary almost sliding off her knees, and then glanced quickly over at Ruby. Had she woken her? But Ruby was still a small hump under her bedclothes, which wasn't surprising. Emmie wasn't sure quite what time it was, but she knew it was very early. When she'd woken up she'd almost been scared to open her eyes, in case it was still the same shadow-haunted darkness, but even through the heavy curtains, a faint light had turned the room an early-morning grey.

Now the light was growing brighter, quite bright enough to see that there was definitely no key hidden in the drawer under the diaries. But this must be the place Mary had meant? Still... It was a long time ago, Emmie thought, pushing the drawer closed with a sigh. Almost thirty years. Who knew what had happened to the key – and to the door, and the garden?

Emmie's heart jumped. Was it still a secret? Mary had written that it was the garden beyond the orchard. And that the wall was covered in ivy – that was the dark-leaved stuff. Mr Sowerby had said so. Emmie knew where it was. She could go and see.

Perhaps Arthur and Joey had already found it, Emmie thought with a sharp jolt of disappointment. They had climbed the trees, after all – perhaps they had looked over into the secret garden.

She tried to remember the ivy-covered wall along the path. Had she seen a door? She had been into the kitchen gardens; that was where she'd seen Mr Sowerby. She was almost sure that she had walked through all three – but she had kept away from the orchard, as Arthur and Joey had been there.

She would go and look today. Maybe even now before breakfast. No one had said that they couldn't go out early, Emmie reasoned to herself, slipping out of bed again, and dressing as quietly as she could.

She padded down the passageway barefooted, just as she had done the night before – there was no wind howling at the windows now, the storm had blown itself out, and she could see the pearly sky was deepening to blue.

Emmie glanced up at the little staircase again,

frowning. Perhaps it was the way the chimneys were built, that the wind made strange noises down them. In the daylight, the whimpering sounds seemed unlikely. Emmie shook off the memory of those haunting little cries, and stepped cautiously down the side stairs. The key was in the door, a heavy black iron key that made her think of Mary, and the door to the secret garden. Emmie's fingers slipped on it in her eagerness, and she hauled it open, dragging on her shoes and dashing out down the gravelled path, forgetting to be quiet. She shoved through the shrubbery gate and ran as fast as she could through the trees, the shortest way down to the long path outside the walled gardens. This was where Mary had described the door, Emmie was sure of it. It was where she had been skipping when she saw the wind blow away the ivy.

As she came on to the path alongside the great wall, Emmie stopped running. It seemed too important to run – she couldn't come at the secret garden in a rush. She almost felt as though she needed to creep up on it, in case it had disappeared, like something in a fairy tale.

She came towards the end of the wall, where Mary had written that the ivy was thicker and more overgrown than anywhere else, and looked round furtively. But everywhere was deserted this early in the morning. Perhaps she was the only one awake. The ivy still hung over the wall in a great heavy curtain, and there *was* more of it here. Emmie could feel her heart suddenly thumping all through her as she stepped on to the flower bed, behind a gnarled lilac tree, and felt under the ivy for the door handle. The ivy rustled against her fingers, and the flowers smelled odd, but she hardly cared – for there under her fingers was a smooth brass doorknob, worn silken with use.

Emmie stopped, rubbing her fingers over the smooth metal. Would it open? Would she be able to get inside without the key? She stood hesitating, trails of ivy draped over and around her, not quite daring to turn the handle in case she was still shut out.

At last she let out a sharp, frightened gasp, and wrenched the handle round. The door creaked a little, and caught, and then opened inwards. Emmie ducked right beneath the trails of ivy and stepped into the secret garden.

A rush of scent and twittering and early morning wet grass wrapped around her.

Mary's description of the garden, wild and overgrown and winter-grey, was still strong in her mind, so what struck her all at once was the brightness and the scent of roses. They had not been dead, after all... They still poured themselves from tree to tree in great trailing curtains, and there seemed to be flowers all around her.

Emmie closed the green door and leaned against it, staring around. The garden looked to be about the same size as the kitchen gardens – perhaps it had been built as one, originally, before it was made into a rose garden? But instead of neatly edged beds, full of late lettuces, there were trees all around the walls, apples and peaches and plums, with just enough of each still on the branches for Emmie to see what they were. Between the trees there was a lawn, but this wasn't a smooth carpet of green, like the terrace that ran down to the fish pond. Instead the grass was broken up here and there with clusters of tall evergreen bushes, each one like a frame for a carved stone seat, or a statue, or a huge urn spilling over with flowers.

She wandered breathlessly under the arches, reaching up every so often to touch a rose, laughing as they shed their petals on her face and shoulders. The summer had been long, and hot, and many of the roses had finished flowering already, with just the odd late blossom left here and there, but Emmie would have found it hard to believe that there could be more flowers. She seemed to be wrapped up in them, roses overhead, and spilling out of the flower beds a great mass of lilies, so strongly scented that she could almost see the perfume in the air.

The early morning sun was brighter now, warming her through the skimpy sleeves of her cardigan. Emmie smiled to herself, and began to whirl around, spinning like a top, lifting her chin and closing her eyes, so she saw only a rich orange sunglow under the lids. The scents of the garden swirled around her and she spun on until she staggered, dizzy and giggling. Then she slowed down, stepping gently from foot to foot as she twirled, listening to the hum of bees, and the tiny birds twittering in amongst the creepers.

The garden couldn't be a secret now, Emmie realized, as she stopped to lean dizzily against a great tree: a tree that had no leaves of its own, but was so wrapped in climbing roses that it seemed more alive than ever. Mary had described a garden that had been abandoned. Now the grass had been trimmed, and although the roses still scrambled wildly everywhere, they had been shaped around the trees and statues. Even though the door had been hidden, it was no longer locked.

"She let other people in," Emmie whispered to herself regretfully. She had so wanted it to be her secret too. She could have hidden herself away.

But she could still come here, she decided. It *was* only hers now, so early in the morning. There would be other times too. And if someone came, it wasn't as if there was nowhere to hide. Emmie smiled to herself, riffling the petals of a fat, crimson-purple rose. The petals were layered together so tightly that even her small fingers wouldn't slip between them.

It wasn't a secret garden any more – but it could still be her garden full of secrets.

Over the next few days, Emmie went to the garden whenever she could, prowling around and looking at the statues, and the flowers. Sometimes she pinched away the dying flowers on the roses – not because she knew it was the right thing to do, but because she didn't like the faded colours, and the way the browned flowers smelled so sickly sweet. She piled up the dead flowers in a corner behind one of the statues, so they didn't show.

The robin watched her, often perching in the trees above her head and twittering, she thought with approval. "You like me being here, don't you?" she said to him once, hurrying past with an old basket full of rose heads. She had found the basket behind one of the glasshouses, and she'd brought a little pair of sewing scissors too, that she'd found abandoned in the schoolroom. They were good for snipping away the flowers, and no one missed them. The real garden tools were all locked away in the sheds.

The robin came closer to her every day – once, he even sat on the basket. She was almost sure that he had his home in an overgrown corner of the garden. There was a tiny statue of a boy playing a flute, almost hidden by creepers, their leaves orange and golden now that autumn was coming. In the spring, it would be the perfect place for a nest.

On the days she'd been in the garden, Emmie came back to the house for breakfast in a hurry, forgetful of the time and with petals in her hair, and somehow the garden made it easier to put up with Arthur's smirking face or Ruby whining for help with her buttons. She went back there in her head, wandering among the lilies and roses, or stretching out on the sun-warmed stone of the seats. Then she would surprise Ruby by twirling her around and hugging her once the dress was all buttoned up.

Often Emmie just sat, curled up under the great dead tree. She leaned against the seamed bark, gazing round and imagining it all as Mary had seen it, dark and dead in winter. How long would she and the others be here? No one had said. Would she see the garden in winter too? Emmie was still reading the diary, but being out in the gardens so much made her tired, and she never managed to puzzle her way through much of the ornate handwriting before she fell asleep.

Walking about the garden and admiring the flowers made her wonder what all their names were, and if there was someone she could ask. She would have liked to talk to the gardener with the false leg, Mr Sowerby, but even though she saw him again in the kitchen gardens, she didn't go up to him. How could she explain what she wanted to know, and why? What if he realized what she was doing, and told her that garden was private, and she mustn't go in there again? She still would, but it would take the shine off her secret. Besides, Emmie's stomach squirmed when she thought of the way she had looked at his face. She didn't know how to say she hadn't meant to grimace. Or that she'd only meant it for a fraction of a second. She wasn't sure that there was a proper way to say that.

The garden felt more like it belonged to her every day, with every fallen leaf she gathered up. Emmie hated the thought that one morning she might walk in, and find someone else already there. For the first few mornings, she peered fearfully around the door, trying to hear if there were voices, or if one of the gardeners was whistling inside. But no one seemed to know about the garden, even though she occasionally saw that more deadheading had been done than she could have managed, that the heavy-headed lilies had been carefully tied up with twine, the leaves falling from the apple trees had been raked away. The garden was loved, but no one ever seemed to go in it. No one except Emmie, sneaking in like a thief.

Until the golden, sunny afternoon when she sauntered out after they'd had lessons, and saw Mrs

Craven walking down the long path by the brick wall, with a letter in her hand.

Emmie knew where she was going – she knew, but she had to watch anyway, biting her lip, wishing and wishing that it wasn't going to happen. But it did. Almost without looking, Mrs Craven put out her hand to sweep the ivy away, and then slipped in through the green door. She left it standing open, as if she didn't care whether the garden were secret or not. Emmie stood on the path by the lilac tree, watching and waiting, her fists clenched, and her teeth bared like an angry little cat. She stood there for half an hour, hating. When she heard footsteps in the garden, she pressed herself back against the wall behind the lilac, and tried not to snarl as Mrs Craven sauntered by in a trail of some sweet, flowery perfume. It made Emmie want to cough.

As soon as Mrs Craven had disappeared round the corner of the path, Emmie sneaked back in. She expected that somehow the garden would look different – that she would be able to see the way it had been spoiled. But the roses were blooming just the same.

Emmie lay down on the grass behind a veil of small pink roses. Mrs Craven had been sitting on a bench in one of the alcoves, and most of the time she had had her eyes closed – Emmie had looked. She hadn't picked any flowers, or even walked around. But still the secret garden felt different, as though it had woken up from a dream, or Emmie had. Misselthwaite was Mrs Craven's house, and her husband's, and David and Jack's. Not one part of it was Emmie's. It never had been.

"I shouldn't ever have pretended it was my garden. . ." she whispered to herself, pressing her face into the crook of her elbow. She had – in her head she had moved one of the statues that she didn't like. She had imagined planting a great drift of purple daisies in and out of the white lilies, and building a little summerhouse with its walls all made of roses and the sweet honeysuckle she'd seen, clambering up a sunny patch of wall by the green door.

She had pictured herself curled up in a chair, a wicker chair like the ones that stood on the terrace in front of the grand rooms of the house, covered in cushions. Golden honey-smelling flowers grew over her head, thrumming with bees. Lucy had been stretched out asleep on her lap, a safe, contented Lucy who belonged, like she did. They had been happy.

And now it was all gone. Lucy had never even been in the garden. Lucy was probably *destroyed*, like that boy had said. She didn't even have a cat curled up with her on a rusty old fire escape any more, let alone in a house made of flowers. It was all a silly, empty daydream. Emmie wailed, forgetting to be quiet, and secret. It didn't matter anyway. The garden was broken. The secret was gone.

She wept, tears streaming down her cheeks and trickling into the grass.

"Lass. Lass. Look at me."

Emmie rolled over, gasping, as someone caught her arm. She hadn't even heard him coming.

"Whatever's the matter?"

It was the gardener, Mr Sowerby, looking down at her with the unscarred side of his face pink and worried.

Emmie wanted to howl again, and run – but she couldn't. If she did that, he might think it was because she was frightened of him, and she wasn't, she just desperately wished that everyone would leave her alone. She pulled away from him, and huddled over, curled into a ball with her face hidden in her knees.

"Did someone hurt thee?"

Emmie managed to shake her head, as much as she could curled up. "Go away," she sobbed. "Leave me alone."

He was silent for a while – so silent that she almost wondered if he'd gone. But when she looked up, he had settled himself uncomfortably on a little white bench under the rose arch. He was rubbing his leg as though it hurt.

"Isn't that a false leg?" Emmie asked, shakily. "It can't be hurting. You can't even feel if you rub it."

"Tell that to th' leg," he muttered. "Now, what's making thee take on so?" Then his gaze sharpened, and he stopped massaging his leg and leaned forward to look at her properly. "Is it you? Been deadheading the roses?"

Emmie dropped her head again. "Wasn't it right? They were brown. I wanted to make room for the others, the little ones that were just opening out."

He chuckled, such a surprising noise that Emmie looked up and stared at him. He had bright blue eyes, she noticed, now that she was looking past the scars. Sky-blue eyes, and dark red hair curling out from under his cap.

"Tha's been doing a grand job of it, lass. Don't tha' worry."

"I didn't know where to put the brown bits," Emmie admitted. "I hid them behind the statue over there. That one of the girl with the silly smile." Then she sighed, rubbing her hands across her sore eyes. Now even that secret was gone.

He nodded, and then leaned back against the bench, drawing a piece of wood and a knife from his pocket. He opened the knife out, and began to shave tiny flecks of wood away, shaping something. He didn't talk to Emmie, but he must have sensed her edging closer to the bench.

"What is it?" she asked at last. She couldn't quite see – the carving was tiny.

He opened up his hand and showed her, and Emmie laughed. The robin was peeking out at her, head on one side, tail-feathers practically twitching.

"It's the robin – the one who lives in this garden, isn't it?" She reached out one finger, wanting to stroke it, and then looked up at him, pleadingly. "If I was to tell you what she looked like, do you think you could make a cat? I'd do more helping in the garden, whatever you wanted. You'd just have to show me, I promise I'd do it."

"A cat, is it?"

"Maybe only a kitten. I don't think she ever had enough food to grow much."

"Like thee, then."

Emmie sighed. "I'm fatter now. I gave some of my food to Lucy. That's my cat's name. I didn't mind." Her voice shook. "She'd love it here. They keep giving us milk. I'd smuggle it out to her. And the porridge, it's nicer here."

"A real little cat, this is then?" He was frowning now, and Emmie nodded. She thought he was cross.

"I never wanted to leave her! I had her all ready to go in a basket; I wanted to bring her with us, away from the bombs, but Miss Dearlove said she was disgusting, and she wasn't, she was a love. She was all mine."

Suddenly she couldn't bear his eyes on her, and she stumbled up, grabbing at the bench, meaning to run away. But he caught at her hand. "Stay. Tell me about tha' little cat."

His voice was so gentle and coaxing that Emmie paused, half-ready to run, like a little wild thing. His hand was rough from working in the garden, but he wasn't holding her tight. If she'd pulled hard, she could easily have got away. But she didn't.

She stayed, like the robin, who'd perched on the gardener's shoulder.

"Tell us about her..." He patted the bench, and Emmie settled in the corner, drawing up her knees.

"She's black," Emmie began. Then she closed her eyes, trying to make a picture of Lucy in her head. It was getting harder and harder to see her. "Black all over, and quite thin. Arthur and Joey said she was skinny," she added, and her scowl came back, just for a moment, drawing two deep lines above her nose. Then she sighed, and her face smoothed out again. "Even her whiskers are black. The only colour's her eyes, and they're yellowy-green. They shine. They even glow, sometimes, when it's dark on the fire escape."

"That's where thee found her, then?"

"It's my place," Emmie explained. "No one goes there except for me." She shivered, and opened her eyes to look at him. "No one's in that house now at all. It's empty. I don't know when we'll go back."

"Does tha' miss it?"

Emmie shook her head. "No. I – I like it here..." She said it slowly, as if she were only just working it out for herself. "I love this garden especially," she added. "I thought it was a secret."

She was looking out across the garden, so she didn't see him glance up, his eyes widening.

"A secret?" His voice was wistful, and he glanced up at the covering of roses, and then the neatly cut grass, as if he was seeing something different.

"No one else came. Like the fire escape, only better. Much better." Emmie sighed. "Except that I didn't have Lucy. I don't even know where she is." She wriggled up, and put her hand on his knee. "Do you know the boy who lives here? Jack?"

He nodded.

"He said that cats in London are being destroyed. Because there won't be enough food." Her voice wobbled. "Lucy doesn't eat much. I gave her a bit, and I think Mrs Evans in the kitchen did too. Mostly she took stuff out of bins." She hesitated, not wanting to ask, in case he told her the truth. But then she remembered how the robin had perched on his shoulder, and trusted him. This man understood about creatures, she thought. "Do you think she's still there? What if someone. . ." She couldn't say it.

"Cats is clever," he murmured. "And they likes their own place. She knows where to hide herself away, doesn't she?"

Emmie nodded, remembering the way that Lucy

had appeared on the fire escape, almost out of nowhere. "But there's no one to feed her."

"She'll get by. Is that why tha' were crying? Worrying about th' little cat?"

"I could remember her properly here. I planted a house for her. . ." She looked round at him, suspiciously, in case he were laughing. But he was watching her, his face grave, and remembering.

"Tha' reminds me of another little lass," he said, stretching out his leg as though it ached.

Emmie eyed him curiously, wanting to ask who he meant, but even though he was gazing out across the garden, she didn't think he could see glowing hips of the roses, shining against the clipped yew hedges. It was as though he had forgotten she was there. She watched him silently, seeing his mouth twist in a remembering smile.

Then at last the gardener sighed, and glanced down at her and slapped his knees. "I better get on. Only came in here after I heard thee wailing. Be of good faith, lass. Tha' cat will be waiting for thee, when tha' goes back." He stood up, limping back to the barrow he'd left on the path, and Emmie watched him go. He hadn't his crutch today; his leg must be feeling better.

She turned back sharply as something rustled behind her. Was it the robin again? She peered at the bushes, hoping to see his black eyes glittering among the leaves. But instead, there was a boy, guiltily half-stooping behind the great dead tree.

"You!" Emmie sprang up. "What are you doing? Were you listening? Were you spying on me? Have you been there all this time?"

Jack had looked almost apologetic, when she first saw him, but now he straightened up, and marched out from behind the tree with a haughty expression. "Yes. And I wasn't spying. This is my garden. This is my *house*. I can go anywhere I like."

"I hate you," Emmie snarled. She clenched her fists. If she scratched her nails down his face, as she longed to, she'd be in such trouble. . . "It isn't your garden."

"It's all mine." He waved a lordly hand around at the tree, and the roses. "All of it. You're not to come in here again."

"It isn't yours," Emmie said again, trying to sound sure. "Mr Sowerby said I could be here. You ask him!"

"He is a servant," Jack pronounced grandly. "It's not up to him to say."

"I don't believe you." Emmie shook her head. Jack's mother hadn't spoken about the sullen, lonely gardener in that way at all. "What were you doing, anyway?" Emmie demanded, feeling braver. "Why were you hiding?"

"I wasn't hiding, you just didn't see me." But Jack had gone red, and Emmie knew he was lying. She guessed that he had been in the garden to try and avoid Joey and Arthur. They were bigger than he was, and he hadn't made himself very popular, sniggering in lessons whenever they got the answers wrong.

Jack caught the little smirk on her face, and the red faded out of his cheeks, leaving them pale with fury. "Get out!" he hissed. "Go away! All of you, leave me alone! This is my house!" Then he plunged past, shoving her sideways, and ran out through the green door and on to the path.

Emmie gazed after him, feeling oddly guilty. Jack had spied on her, and tried to tell her she couldn't be in the garden. Then he'd shouted at her, and knocked her into the rose arch. She had a great long scratch down her leg to prove it. So why did she wish that she'd been nicer?

3rd February 1910

I have told my secret. I never thought I would, but Martha's brother Dickon is more like a wild moor animal than a boy. He promises that he will never tell, and I believe him. He's used to keeping all the nests and burrows that he finds out on the moor secret from the other boys. He says they might steal the birds' eggs if he told. So I can trust him.

I went out through the gate from the laurel walk into the wood. I heard whistling and I thought it might be another sort of bird, but it was a boy, playing on a wooden pipe. He made me remember the snake charmers in India, but he was playing to two rabbits instead, and a bird that's called a pheasant, and a little red squirrel in the tree above his head. They went so close, the rabbits were sitting by his feet.

He had brought the seeds and the garden tools that Martha asked him to buy with the money my uncle gave me. He was explaining how I should plant them, but then he said it would be better to show me, and where was my garden? I didn't know what to say. But I liked him, he smiled so. Perhaps he had charmed me with his pipe-playing too. I took him into the garden. I wanted *someone to tell me if the roses were still alive, and they are! A few are brown and grey all through but most of them are wick – this is the word that means they are green and alive inside. We are going to make the garden wake up properly – it needs the weeds digging up and all the dead wood cutting away from the rose trees. Dickon says that when they all flower in the summer there will be fountains of roses. I cannot wait to see.*

4th February 1910

Yesterday was the strangest day. I have spent so many weeks at Misselthwaite, hardly seeing anyone. Then in one day I meet Dickon, and I am summoned to see my uncle, and in the night of the same day, I find out who it is who has been crying.

There is a boy here, and no one ever told me. They have been keeping it a secret, because he made them. He doesn't like anyone to see him, or know about him. He has been very ill, and he says that he is going to die before he grows up. He is certainly very pale and ill-looking. Martha knew about him all the time and never told me! It's no wonder that she was so panicked when I said I had heard another child cry. She tried to tell me that it was the scullery maid crying because her tooth hurt, but I knew that wasn't the truth. I am not angry with Martha, though. All the servants thought that they would be sent away if they ever spoke about him.

I told him about the garden – not that I have really found it, just that it might be there. I didn't mean to tell, but it's so much in my mind that I let the secret out without thinking. He said that he would make the gardeners tell him where it was, and I thought I had ruined everything. But he liked the thought of a secret garden, where only we could go. I said that perhaps, perhaps, we might find the door.

I went back to Colin's room this afternoon; he made Martha bring me. We talked and talked and I told him about Dickon. In the middle of us talking and laughing together, the housekeeper, Mrs Medlock, and the doctor came in. They were so surprised to see Colin sitting up and cheerful that I almost laughed out loud. The doctor stopped like a statue and nearly tripped Mrs Medlock over. I was worried that Mrs Medlock would be angry with me again, like she was when I came too close to Colin's rooms before. I understand now why she dragged me away. But Colin told them both that I was his cousin, and that he liked me. He likes me! He is very bad-tempered and ill, but then I am bad-tempered too, I suppose.

Martha, Ben Weatherstaff, Dickon, Colin and the robin. Five friends.

"Emmie. Emmie."

Emmie turned over, murmuring in her sleep, and then shivered. She had two jumpers on over her nightdress, and a pair of huge woolly socks, but she was still cold. It had been almost too cold to read Mary's diary the evening before; she had managed only a few pages before her fingers froze.

"What is it?" she asked Ruby, peering grumpily at the little girl from under her nest of blankets. For the last few days, Emmie had only felt warm when she was asleep.

"I'm cold," Ruby said pleadingly. "Can I get in with you?"

Emmie eyed her for a second. Ruby's face looked pinched with cold in the candlelight, and she was shivering. "Why haven't you got your blankets round you? Don't stand there like that, the floor's freezing. Fetch your blankets, come on. And get in fast!"

Ruby scurried obediently to strip her bed, and appeared back at Emmie's bedside looking wider than she was tall, wound in at least three blankets. She scrambled in next to the older girl, and Emmie stretched the extra covers over the two of them like a tent. She could hardly breathe, but it was better than being cold.

There was frost on the inside of the windows again, she expected. And the snow was piled up around the window frames so they could hardly see out. The garden had been smoothed out into a strange landscape of lumps and hills, with paths cut through by the few gardeners who were left.

At first Emmie had thought that winters in Yorkshire must always be like this, but Miss Sowerby promised them it wasn't so. This was the coldest winter there had been in years. There were five-foot drifts out on the moor, and most of the estate workers had temporarily moved into the Manor. It was easier to keep everyone warm in one place.

"Tell me again about the fish," Ruby whispered, snuggling up to Emmie.

Emmie shuddered as Ruby's icy nose pressed against her cheek. "Again?"

"Please, Emmie..."

Emmie gave a sleepy groan, and wrapped her arm around Ruby. The littler girl was like a hot water bottle.

Ruby was supposed to stay close to the house with Miss Rose and the other younger children when they went outside, but the five-year-old was good at slipping away. She loved the huge pond, and she spent hours watching the fish – even though she'd been told she mustn't play by the water. Miss Rose was terrified that she'd fall in.

A few weeks after they'd arrived at Misselthwaite, Emmie had gone to admire the fish, and found Ruby there too. She was crouched at the very edge of the pool, peering down into the water. Beside her on the stone slabs was a pile of breadcrumbs.

Emmie was about to march over and tell the little girl to get back to her own place, but then she realized that if she came up behind Ruby and surprised her, she'd probably fall into the pond, and Emmie would be the one blamed for it.

So she sat down next to her instead, and threw one of Ruby's crumbs into the water. A glowing orange fish surged up to snatch it, and Ruby looked round.

"You aren't supposed to be here," Emmie pointed out.

"I like feeding the fish. They're funny."

"Miss Rose is probably looking for you."

Ruby shrugged, and her mouth straightened into a sulky line. "Not a baby," she muttered. "Sam the gardener saw me feeding the fish, and he said it saved him a job. There's some special fish food; he said he'd show me where it is, if I promised I'd be careful. He's really busy. I'm *helping*." Her bottom lip wobbled, and Emmie nodded quickly.

"All right then! Don't start that." Ruby probably was helping – they all were, now. Arthur and Joey had picked the fruit in the orchard. Emmie helped Mr Sowerby in the secret garden, and in the kitchen gardens too. He'd asked her – and he'd even dug out an ancient pair of Wellington boots that almost fit, so she could dig without caking her sandals in mud. Miss Rose and Miss Dearlove took turns helping with the cooking. Emmie expected that before long they'd all be eating in the servants' hall, to save work. Four of the gardeners had already gone to join the army and several of the maids had left to work in factories building weapons. Even the smaller children helped with sweeping the floors, and Mrs Craven was talking about shutting up some of the rooms, covering everything in dust sheets, until... No one was really sure until what.

"Please, Emmie. Tell me what the fish are doing?" Ruby whispered, breathing warm, damp breath into Emmie's ear.

Emmie started, blinking back from her vague half-dream of that day by the water. She'd almost fallen back to sleep, and she gave a regretful little groan as she realized all over again how cold it was.

"All right." She yawned, and tried to remember the story that had comforted Ruby the week before, when she'd run down to the pool, and seen that the patchy covering of ice was solid – so thick that this time it didn't break when she tapped it. She had been distraught, certain that the fish would all freeze to death. The panicked look on her face had made Emmie think of Lucy, tearing open the old memories all over again. "The fish are down at the bottom of the pool, sleeping," she murmured, and she felt Ruby snuggle up against her side. "It's cold and dark, but the fish don't mind. They're sleeping, dreaming of the sunshine. Every so often they flicker their fins, just a little, to keep themselves warm."

"Tell about the gold sparkling," Ruby whispered.

Emmie smiled to herself, proud that Ruby had remembered her story. "Even though it's so dark under the ice, the fish can see each other's golden scales glittering, and that reminds them that the sun will come back and melt the ice in the springtime."

She yawned, and added, "And tomorrow we'll go and sweep the snow off the top of the pool, and take that old football out of the ice, to let the air in. And deep down at the bottom of the pool the fish will all sniff, and say, *Smells like snow again*. And they'll just flip their tails once, and go back to sleep."

Ruby chuckled, wriggling delightedly at the thought of the little squeaky fishy voices.

"Now go to sleep," Emmie mumbled. "S'late."

Chapter Six

"I found them! I found them!" Emmie raced through the kitchen garden, yelling with delight, skidding and sliding on the icy brick paths until she almost crashed into Mr Sowerby raking a patch of earth.

He straightened up clumsily, staring down at her and grinning. "What did tha' find?"

Emmie panted. It was a good day, she could tell. He was smiling, and he hadn't his crutch. She no longer looked at his scars, they were just as much a part of him as his heavy boots, and velveteen waistcoat, but there were days when she could tell from the set of his shoulders that it was best to run on by.

Emmie put her hand on his arm and looked up

at him pleadingly. "Come and see? Please? It's a good thing, you'll be happy."

He shook his head at her. "Another one as wants me to be happy. Tha' and Mrs Craven. Tha' would have me dancing." But he propped the rake against the wall and limped after her, while she skipped backwards in front of him, beckoning and giggling to herself.

"I've been looking for so long," Emmie explained. "I almost didn't believe you." She ran ahead of him along the path to the secret garden, and then came back to grab his hand and hurry him after her. She hadn't listened to Jack telling her not to go in there. The gardens belonged to the gardener, more than to one spoiled boy, Emmie thought. Mr Sowerby needed her to help, anyway, now that most of the gardeners had gone to fight, and it was only him and a couple of elderly men drafted in from the village to look after the huge expanse of gardens around Misselthwaite Manor. There was a chance that the lawns might have to be dug up and planted with vegetables, but Emmie wasn't sure if the gardeners would be able to manage any more.

"Look!" she dragged Mr Sowerby across the

snowy grass to the white bench under the rose arbour, and crouched down, pointing at a clump of white spears, edged in green and just nudging out of the snow. "Look at them! Are these snowdrops, like you said? They don't look like that drawing in the plant catalogue, but they're new. I walked round looking yesterday, and they weren't here then."

"Ah. . . Th' first ones – it's sheltered here." Mr Sowerby reached down, and cupped the flowers in one of his great hands. Emmie watched, holding her breath. "They won't be all th' way out for a couple more days. These are th' buds. They's late, this year. With the snow like it is." He straightened up and looked around the white garden, sighing with pleasure. The sigh eased out of him, like a long-held breath. Then he shook his head, and clapped the snow from his gloves. "Crocuses soon. Primroses out in th' lanes, and then daffodils. Ah, it'll be a sight, lass. Daffies as far as tha' can see, there'll be."

Emmie stared at the snowy hummocks where the roses had been, and sighed. Mary had talked about all those in her diary, thousands and thousands of green spears, pointing to the sky. She and Dickon had dug all around them, clearing away the choking grass. But the snow was so thick, she couldn't imagine the garden fragrant and green again. "I can't see it. I don't think the snow's ever going away. It's been weeks. And you said we'd have the snowdrops in January!"

The gardener snorted. "Can't always be right, lass. Worst winter for forty year, they do say. Them poor snowdrops is doing their best. They can't show through a foot of snow, can they?"

"S'pose not." Emmie sighed. The snow had been fun, at first – Jack had a sledge, and he had even made a temporary peace with Joey and Arthur, as it was more fun if there was someone to push. Emmie had a few goes, but she and Jack were still pretending that the other one didn't exist, which made it hard to go shrieking down a snow slope with him. Emmie had slipped away after a while. She helped Ruby and the other little ones skid around on two old metal tea trays from the kitchen instead, squealing and tumbling and tipping each other over.

But now the snow just meant that every time they went outside they came back wet, and everyone had chilblains, itching and burning on their fingers and toes. The whole house, huge as it was, seemed to smell of damp wool. Clothes horses were spread in front of every fire, sucking up the warmth before it got into the rooms. There was a lot less snow than there had been – the road from Thwaite was clear again – but the gardens were still wrapped in a white stillness. Even the robin seemed quieter than usual – whenever Emmie saw him he was fluffed out and grumpy-looking, as though the cold was getting to him too.

"Emmie! Emmie! Where are you? You have to come! Emmie!"

"That's Arthur yelling. . ." Emmie turned to look anxiously at the wall that bordered the path. The garden wasn't a complete secret, like it had been for Mary that spring and summer so many years before, but the door was still hidden. It was her refuge still. She didn't want to show Arthur the door under the ivy.

"Let him go by," Mr Sowerby murmured. "He'll be in th' laurel walk in a moment. Then tha' can dart out and run after him."

Emmie nodded, and crunched quietly over the snow to the green door, leaning against it and listening. Then she eased the door open, and slipped out on to the path, with a quick wave to the gardener. Mr Sowerby stood there, tucking his hands under his arms for warmth, and smiling after her. Then he began to limp slowly in her footsteps to the door.

"What is it?" Emmie called, running after Arthur, hissing as her rubber boots skidded on the ice.

Arthur was hanging over the gate to the wood, staring out as if he thought she might have gone that way.

"I'm not that stupid," Emmie said sharply. "There's still drifts out there that could half-bury us."

"The road's clear!" Arthur seized her hand. "You've got to come back to the house. Mr Craven's come home on leave. Lieutenant Craven, he is now."

"So?" Emmie frowned, and then looked hopeful. Now that butter and sugar had been rationed, even the plainest cake was a treat. She couldn't see any other reason she should be interested in Lieutenant Craven's movements. Except that she was a little curious to see Jack's father. "Does that mean there's cake?"

"No, stupid. He wants to see you. Come on. I said I'd fetch you, he's waiting."

He tugged at her hand, and began to run back

along the path through the shrubbery. Emmie followed, still protesting.

"But why? He doesn't even know who I am."

"He does," Arthur called back over his shoulder. "I saw him; I saw the car and I wanted to know who he was. I was in the hall, watching. He said, did I know where Emmie was, and could I fetch you. Straight off. He knew your name all right."

They reached the side door, stopping to knock the snow off their boots, and then peeled off their layers of coats and scarves.

Emmie stared anxiously at her reddened fingers, sore with cold, wondering if she had done something wrong. *I can't think what. Why else would he want to see me, though?* She had Lieutenant Craven in her head as the tall hero that Jack obviously worshipped – she had seen that even from the few words the boy grudgingly spoke during lessons.

Miss Sowerby pounced on her at the top of the stairs, and sighed about her hair, which was all sticking out of its plait, but she didn't make her comb it out. She hurried her along the hallways as eagerly as Arthur had. These were the grander parts of the house, the corridors that the children had never been into. There were thick curtains drawn over most of the windows. Even before the war had started, it had been hard to keep enough servants to care for so large a house. Now, with so many of them gone off to enlist or to do war work, the endless task of opening the curtains and closing them before the blackout had been allowed to lapse. The passages were dim, even in the bright snowlight, and faces glimmered out of dark portraits as Emmie was hurried by.

There was a fire lit in Lieutenant Craven's small study, full of rather dusty velvet-covered chairs. The room had been shut up while he was away; it smelled musty, and there was a fine layer of dust on the huge wooden desk. Standing in front of the fire was a thin, tired-looking man in a dark uniform with glittering buttons.

Emmie was used to seeing Mrs Craven worried about food, or there not being enough blankets, or the possibility that the second gardener's youngest boy had scarlet fever. She had never seen her smile like this before. The light from the window glowed behind her, but her thin, pale face was lit up from inside, so that she shone like the paintings in the passageway.

Emmie ducked her head, embarrassed. She felt as if she were intruding.

"Emmie?" Lieutenant Craven sounded as uncertain as she was.

"Yes," she whispered back, staring at her knitted socks.

"I've brought you something."

Emmie looked up, frowning. "Me? You don't even know who I am."

"Mr Sowerby wrote to me about you. He wrote to me that he'd found you crying in the garden, and you told him about your cat."

Emmie scowled, ashamed for a moment that someone else knew. She had spent so long trying to hide herself away, so no one saw her. Jack had crowed over her tears, and now Mr Sowerby had written it in a letter to this stranger in uniform. She looked up, about to say something angry, but then she caught his eyes. The same dark grey eyes as Jack's, fringed with black lashes.

She clenched her fists, her nails digging into her palms. "I miss her," she muttered, trying to be polite, and only managing fierce instead of angry.

"Emmie, look." Mrs Craven stood up, and put an arm around her shoulders, pushing her gently over to the armchair by the fire. On the chair was a basket – a wicker picnic basket, very like the one she had tried to bring Lucy in, months before.

"Is it a cake?" Emmie asked, bewildered.

Lieutenant Craven laughed. "Look and see."

Emmie shook her head stubbornly. He was laughing at her.

He stopped smiling, and came closer, squatting down next to the basket. "Mr Sowerby wrote to me – he told me how you'd fought to bring your little cat. He said the first time he saw you, you looked completely lost, wandering around the gardens as though you'd never seen flowers before." He looked down at the basket, his dark brows drawing together. "You don't understand what it's like for me, to be away from here, Emmie. This is my home. I've lived here always – everything in me is tied up with Misselthwaite, even when I go away. Letters are like a glimpse of home for me; I read them over and over. I could see this lost little girl in my gardens. Even though I'd never met you, I'd read about you so often. I knew you, and I liked you because Mr Sowerby liked you." He smiled to himself. "He knew what he was doing, telling me about you in the garden, and the cat left behind." Lieutenant Craven glanced at the basket, and reached out one hand, as if he was going to pat it – then he drew his fingers back, cautiously.

"I've got a week's leave, that's all, but I had to spend last night in London, as I couldn't get a train till this morning. So I went to the Home – your Miss Dearlove had written to me as well, she's been worried about leaving the building empty – she wanted someone to check that all the windows were secured still. To make sure no one had broken in."

Emmie nodded, still unsure what this had to do with her.

"I walked all round the building, you see. Making sure everything was all right. Into the yard, and up the fire escape."

Emmie gasped, suddenly breathless. She felt like she did that time she'd had a fight with Arthur. He'd pushed her, hard, and she'd smacked against the wall and lost all the air inside.

"Did you see her?" she whispered, forcing the words out.

He nodded. "She must have heard me thumping about on the fire escape. Perhaps she thought I was you." He snorted. "*She* was so quiet that I didn't even notice her until she was on the step below me.

I tried to grab her – goodness knows what I'd have done if I'd caught her. Put her in my pocket?"

"She ran away?" Emmie came closer, putting her hand on his sleeve. "Was she all right? Was she thin?"

He nodded. "Very thin, I'm afraid. So I went back to the hotel, and borrowed a torch, and they managed to find me some fish-paste sandwiches. I told them I'd missed lunch."

"Fish paste?" Emmie echoed, looking at the basket, and wrapping her arms tightly round her middle. She felt as though she was holding herself together, holding everything in. Did he mean what she thought he meant, or was she making up a stupid story again – like the house she'd imagined for herself and Lucy in the garden, her pretty honeysuckle house?

Emmie wanted to run, and tear at the fastenings of the basket. But what if there was only a cake in there after all – or fish-paste sandwiches?

"Mm-hm. I'm glad I thought of it. She was tricky to catch. Though at least it wasn't too hard to see her, against the snow."

"You – you mean it? You're not just teasing me?" Emmie asked, stepping closer.

He snorted, and held out one hand, so she could see the deep red scratch across the back. "I'd be careful when you get her out. She's cross about the basket." He nodded at Emmie. "I sat on that fire escape in the snow with a plate of fish-paste sandwiches, waving them about like a clown."

"And she came back?" Emmie took a step closer.

"It took her a while. She came out from behind the bins in the yard. She didn't want to come anywhere near me, but she couldn't resist the smell of the food. She's very thin. She might leap out when you open the basket, Emmie. She didn't want to go in there at all, and she's been shut up since yesterday afternoon. I didn't dare open it again; I just lifted up the lid a fraction and posted more sandwiches in. I know that sounds cruel," he added apologetically, "but I didn't want to lose her in the hotel, or even worse, in a train. I wouldn't have put it past her to escape at some station in the middle of nowhere."

"Lucy?" Emmie whispered, crouching down in front of the chair. What if it was the wrong cat? What if this was all some stupid joke? Jack would do that, and this was Jack's father. She scowled at the basket, trying not to be too hopeful.

There was no sound, except a faint creaking of the basket, as if something inside had moved, just a little. The darkness behind the strands of wicker shifted slightly.

Emmie smiled, just faintly, almost believing that it was true. She could imagine Lucy, glaring suspiciously through the wickerwork. She was surprised Lieutenant Craven only had one scratch. Carefully, she began to thread the wicker catches back through their loops, and then she lifted the lid, just a little. A pair of green eyes shone out of the shadows of the basket, and Lucy hissed at her.

Emmie sat back on her heels. "It's open," she whispered. "You can come out now." She desperately wanted to throw the lid back and hug Lucy tight, but the little cat had been in the dark for so long.

Lucy had huddled up at the back of the basket, full of distrust, but now she crept forward. A small dark muzzle appeared out of the gap, fringed with black whiskers, and a faint smell of concentrated fish.

"Hello, puss," Emmie said, her voice very low, and calm – like Mr Sowerby talking to the robin.

Lucy edged out a little further, so that all of her small black head was free. She darted a glance sideways at the Cravens, and Emmie was almost sure that she recognized Lieutenant Craven as the person who had stuffed her into the basket. She practically spat.

"It was the only way he could bring you," she explained gently. "I know you didn't like it. But if you come out, you could have some milk." She glanced sideways at Lieutenant Craven. "I'll give her what would be on my bread and milk at teatime; I don't like bread and milk anyway."

"She can have her own allowance of milk," Mrs Craven murmured. "We'll stretch to it. It isn't rationed yet, and anyway, we get it from the farm. And she'll deserve it if she can mouse."

"She did catch a couple of them at the Home," Emmie assured her. "But then she left a dead mouse in one of Mrs Evans's slippers, so nobody was very grateful." She lifted the lid up a little more, and the dark ears flickered. "Lucy... Come out, sweetness... I never thought I'd see you again... I thought someone would take you away, and – and I don't know what." She did, but she wasn't going to say it.

The black cat suddenly erupted out of the basket, hissing, and Lieutenant Craven took several steps backwards, making his wife laugh.

"She's already drawn blood once," he pointed out, tucking his hands behind his back.

Lucy scrabbled and clawed and landed in Emmie's lap, where she sat hunched up and rigid, with her ears laid back, glaring around the room.

"Ssssh, ssssh, puss..." Emmie muttered, spilling out a stream of soothing nonsense words to calm the furious cat down. "It's all right, yes, horrible basket. Shall we put it in the fire, yes, shall we, mmm? I don't mean it," she went on, flicking her eyes sideways to Lieutenant Craven. "Probably you have to give it back. Yes, yes he does..."

"Where did you find a cat basket?" Mrs Craven asked him in a whisper.

"It's a very expensive hamper, *actually*. And I went and bought it at Fortnums, when I realized I'd need something to put her in. What was in it might have to be your Christmas present for the next several years."

Mrs Craven pressed her hand over her mouth, laughing at him.

"And Mr Sowerby can have the basket," Lieutenant Craven added. "If he can get the stink of fish out of it."

Lucy's ears were still flat, but now she was sniffing

cautiously at Emmie's fingers. "It is me," Emmie promised, running one hand down Lucy's back. She could feel the cat's ribs under her dull fur. "You're starving," she whispered, her eyes stinging with tears. She looked round at Lieutenant Craven. "I don't think she'll ever be grateful, but I am. You don't know how much. I think you rescued her just in time; I don't suppose people are throwing away as much food as they did before. She's even skinnier than she used to be. Thank you." Emmie nodded her head to him, almost like a formal little bow. She didn't know how to say it better, but she wished she could.

Lieutenant Craven half-bowed back to her, very smartly. Emmie supposed he was used to doing that sort of thing on ships. "I only wish I could have brought her sooner," he said, smiling. "I worried about her too, when I was on the ship and thinking of you all. Would she go with you now, do you reckon? She doesn't want to be anywhere near me – or the basket."

Emmie ran her hand over Lucy's back again, and then down from behind her ears, so that the thin cat shivered, and stretched a little, and nestled closer. Emmie nodded. "Could I take the basket though? I know she doesn't like it now, but she might want it to hide in. She does like little dark places. I don't think Mr Sowerby would want it really – the smell won't go. Fish paste doesn't." Then she swallowed, pulling Lucy tight under her chin and feeling the soft warmth of her domed head. "I don't have any money."

Lieutenant Craven blinked at her, as though he didn't understand.

"For the basket – or the expensive things you had to buy in it. . ."

"But you've been working in the gardens," Mrs Craven broke in, and Emmie saw her kick her husband, very gently, as if she was telling him something. "The children have been working very hard."

Lieutenant Craven nodded. "Mr Sowerby said that. And with so many of the gardeners called up, he told me you children were a blessing. You've earned a basket. You can owe me the scratch," he added, grinning at her, and Emmie nodded. She knew he was joking, but she didn't care. She did owe him. She knew that.

As she walked away from the study, with Lucy still tense in her arms, Emmie thought about keeping a cat in a house with a hundred rooms. How would she ever know where Lucy was? Emmie waited for her to wriggle and fight and jump away, but Lucy huddled still, as daunted by the huge house as Emmie had been.

Miss Sowerby was polishing a table at the end of the passage, even though as the housekeeper that was a job she wouldn't usually do. Emmie quickened her step, and Miss Sowerby dropped the cloth as soon as Emmie appeared, and beamed at her. "He found th' little cat for you, then?"

"You knew about Lucy too?" Emmie asked, confused. "Did Mr Sowerby tell you?" He was her brother, Emmie supposed. They would talk.

Miss Sowerby peered down at Lucy, cringing in Emmie's arms, and made a soft, chirruping noise to her. "And desperate for someone to love. Go an' show her to Miss Dearlove. Tell her Master Craven brought her for thee. But nicely. Don't tha' smirk."

"I wouldn't," Emmie said quickly. "It's too important. I wouldn't. Miss Sowerby, can I really keep her in the house? She's never been a proper house cat. She doesn't know about … about being clean. What if she makes a mess?"

The housekeeper sighed, and looked thoughtfully

at the two skinny little creatures. "She'll learn, I expect. If she makes a mess, you come t' me, and I'll help thee clean up."

Emmie nodded. She could feel Lucy relaxing a little, the hammering of her heart slowing. She followed Miss Sowerby through the house to the servants' hall, gently murmuring to Lucy about how much she was loved, and how many mice she could catch in the dusty old house.

They came upon Jack in the dim passageway that led to the servants' hall, and the kitchen, clutching a doorstep of bread and dripping. Miss Sowerby clicked her tongue at him.

"You'll spoil tha' dinner!"

But Jack didn't even look at her. He glared at Emmie. "My father came home – he's been away for months – and all he wanted was to talk to *you*."

Emmie glared back. "It was important."

Lucy's whiskers twitched, and she leaned a little out of Emmie's arms, catching the scent of the dripping. Jack stepped back, staring at her wide-eyed.

"Your cat!"

"He found her. Your father did. He had to go to the Home, and he saw Lucy, so he brought her back." She swallowed, trying to think of something nice to say. Jack was horrible, but his father wasn't. "It was very kind of him," she managed primly.

"I don't know why he bothered," Jack muttered angrily, barging past. "That looks more like a rat to me."

"Jack Craven!" Miss Sowerby snapped. "Apologize."

But Jack was already gone, racing up the passageway and slamming the door at the bottom of the stairs. Miss Sowerby sighed, and ushered Emmie on into the servants' hall.

"There she is!" Arthur swung round from the table as he saw them at the door. "What did he want? Emmie! Your cat!"

"Lieutenant Craven found her," Emmie said simply. She gave Miss Dearlove a pleading look. "He went and found her, Miss. Mr Sowerby the gardener wrote to him and said about me and Lucy. He knew I missed her. Lieutenant Craven brought her all the way here in a hamper." She bit her lip, and forced herself to sound humble. "Please may I keep her?" Deep in Lucy's fur, her fingers were crossed. If Miss Dearlove said no, it didn't matter. Emmie was keeping her anyway. And Miss Dearlove could hardly send her back. But it was the right thing, to ask. For Lucy she'd do it, however much she hated to speak sweetly and beg.

Emmie buried her face in Lucy's fur, and looked sideways at the matron, trying to see what she would do. Miss Dearlove's fingers clenched on the soup spoon she was holding, and then she dropped it in her bowl with a clinking sound.

"He went to the Home?" she murmured. "I wrote to him. . ."

"He checked all around." Emmie nodded. "He said the windows weren't broken. And then he sat on the fire escape. He had sandwiches."

Miss Dearlove shook her head wearily. "You'll have to keep her then. He's the owner of the house, Emmie. If he fetched her, I can't tell you no."

Emmie swallowed, and didn't look at her. She couldn't stop herself looking happy, and she was sure Miss Dearlove would think she was being rude. "Thank you, Miss Dearlove." And then she added quickly, "I promise I'll keep her out of your way, Miss."

"You'd better see if Mrs Evans and Mrs Martin have got anything you can feed her."

Emmie nodded, and hurried out towards the kitchens.

"Miss Sowerby told us, Emmie," Mrs Evans

surged over to cluck at Lucy. "Isn't she thin, poor little dear. . ."

Mrs Martin looked at Lucy doubtfully. "She's not much bigger than a mouse herself. Is tha' sure she can hunt?"

"That mouse was in my slippers, Betty, I'm telling you," Mrs Evans assured her grimly. "Sit down here, Emmie, I'll find her a saucer for some milk, and you eat this soup." She rubbed one work-reddened finger under Lucy's chin. "Go on, girl. You'll have to let go of her some time."

"I still can't really believe I've got her," Emmie admitted, in a halting whisper.

Mrs Evans fetched a cracked saucer from the back of a shelf, and went into the larder to pour in the milk. She put it down next to the table, and Emmie ran her hand down Lucy's fur again, and loosened her fingers. She waited for Lucy to spring away, but the cat darted her head sideways, and licked at the fur on her shoulder. It was as if she was pretending not to notice the milk – or at any rate, not straight away.

After a few seconds of washing, she peered down at the milk, and jumped elegantly from Emmie's knee to sniff at it, and then she began to lap furiously, forgetting all her dignity, and splashing her whiskers in the saucer.

At last she licked at the china, her little tongue rasping over the glaze, and then stood up, arching her back high. She licked the drops of milk off her whiskers, and stalked across the kitchen. Emmie held her breath, but all Lucy did was jump on to the basket chair that Mrs Martin kept for the moments she could sit down. Lucy sat in the middle of the basket chair, staring around coolly.

"Look at her!" Mrs Martin laughed "Cheeky little beggar! Rulin' the roost, she'll be, give her a day or so."

"You don't think she'll run away?" Emmie said hopefully.

Mrs Evans gave a sniff. "Nonsense. She knows she's fallen on her feet, look at her. Cat knows which side her bread's buttered, Emmie."

Emmie giggled. "She does like bread and butter."

"She likes everything," Mrs Evans muttered. "I remember. Mind, Emmie, she's not to get into the larder."

Lieutenant Craven had only a week before he had to go back to his ship, the destroyer HMS *Grafton*, which was moored in Harwich, further down the north coast from Misselthwaite. From there they sailed out to patrol the water between Germany and Holland, hunting for merchant ships carrying materials that Germany could use for the war effort.

Emmie met him, several times, tramping around the gardens in his Navy-issue oilskins and boots, almost always with Mrs Craven's arm wrapped in his. Jack darted about beside them, dashing off and then back again, as if there was a string holding them all together, and he couldn't be pulled too far away from his father.

Lieutenant Craven smiled at her each time, and Emmie thought he would like to stroke Lucy, but the little cat laid her ears flat whenever she saw him. She felt like saying thank you again – or doing something to show how grateful she was. But it was hard, with Jack scowling at her. She always just smiled, and hurried past.

A couple of days after Lieutenant Craven had arrived, Emmie slipped into the secret garden to look at the snowdrops again, Lucy padding after her and shivering. She pulled up short, finding him sitting on the bench under the rose arch, with Mr Sowerby beside him.

"How is she?" he called, nodding at Lucy.

"She doesn't like the snow much. She keeps shaking it off her paws." Emmie looked around the garden rather sadly. "Don't you wish you could see it better? It's mostly still under snow."

He snorted a little. "If I can see it in my tiny quarters on the ship, how much easier do you think it is when I'm actually here?" He closed his eyes, and pulled his hands out of the deep pockets of his coat to point. "Yellow climbing rose up that wall. Blue and white columbines in the bed underneath, and the pink oriental poppies round the statue of Atalanta. Pink roses around the sundial, white roses up the wall behind, and those little pink things I can't remember the name of across the front." He opened his eyes again, and looked at her. He was smiling, but he still looked sad. "I could go all around the garden. I see it all the time."

Emmie nodded, and reached down to pick up Lucy, who was prowling miserably around her feet. The cat followed her whenever she went outside, but the melting snow left her wet, and skinnier than ever. Emmie had even asked Miss Sowerby if she could clean something, so as to have a job indoors.

"Poor little creature." Lieutenant Craven leaned over to look at her. "She looks fatter though."

"Little minx," Mr Sowerby said coaxingly, holding the back of his hand so Lucy could sniff at it.

Lucy wriggled, and sprang out of Emmie's arms to walk along the arm of the bench, and rub her face against Mr Sowerby's damp sleeve.

Emmie watched, trying not to feel jealous. Mrs Craven had told her that Mr Sowerby was an animal charmer, but until now she had only seen him with the robin. Her face set, and she took a step back, not even realizing that she was doing it.

Lucy whisked back along the arm, and padded quickly after her, laying her ears back as the cold of the snow hit her paws. She rubbed the edge of her chin along the top of Emmie's wellington boot, and purred, a deep, thrumming sound that was almost too loud for such a thin body. It was the first time Emmie had heard her purr. Not even back in London had she done it. Emmie stared at her, and then at Mr Sowerby, her mouth open in surprise. Then she crouched down in the snow, and ran her mittens over Lucy's back, again and again, while the little cat went on purring.

Mr Sowerby chuckled. "Don't tha' fear, little lass. She belongs to thee."

2nd June 1910

Colin is making a scientific experiment. He says there must be magic in the garden – I am sure he is right, I felt it, even from the first time that I opened the door. Perhaps it was because Colin's mother loved the garden so much, or because it was left on its own for so long. But the magic of growing things is in the garden, our Secret Garden. It does make something out of nothing, as Colin says. The garden is full of great silken poppies that Dickon and I planted, but they were the tiniest little black grains before. I remember tipping them out of the paper packet into my hand, and thinking I would lose them all.

If the magic can do that, then it must be able to help Colin grow strong. Already he can stand up. He was sure he would never be able to walk, but now he can manage a few steps. If we believe, then perhaps the magic will make it come true. He will live to grow up.

I felt the magic, I know I did. It was in the green light shimmering through the leaves, and the humming sound of the bees. Already the garden has made me stronger, and happier. It must heal Colin too.

"It's doing it again." Emmie sat up cautiously – Lucy was curled behind her knees, and she didn't want to push her off the bed by accident. "That noise."

Lucy stood up, and stretched, and marched up Emmie's legs to nuzzle at her face.

"You're so heavy. Greedy puss," Emmie murmured lovingly. Lucy probably wouldn't ever be a big cat, but after a month of proper meals, there was a covering over her bones, and her fur was almost glossy. She looked loved.

A thin, sobbing cry made Lucy lay back her ears, and Emmie gasped. "You heard that too! It is real, then. . . I haven't heard it for weeks, and the last time I almost decided I'd just made it up, or it was half a dream." She glanced over at Ruby, but the little girl was fast asleep. Emmie picked Lucy up, snuggling the cat against her shoulder, and wrapped a blanket round them both like a shawl. "I can't manage you and a blanket and a candle," she muttered, looking at the night light doubtfully. "But I think it's starting to get light. A little bit."

Even so, the passageway was almost entirely dark, and Emmie shuffled along with one hand to the wooden panelling, feeling for doors, and the gap where the stairs were. "It is real," she muttered every so often, as she heard another stifled whimper, and Lucy twitched. "It's real. It's not a ghost, and I'm not making it up. This isn't a dream." She turned slowly, as the crying came again – she had thought it was coming from the passage that led off sideways from theirs, but now she was almost sure the noise was above them, although she didn't quite see how. For one horrible moment, she looked up to the white ceiling, expecting to see a hunched, dark shape crouched above her, and howling. But there wasn't, and Emmie shook her head crossly. That was a stupid idea out of a nightmare, or a ghost story, like the ones Arthur and Joey tried to scare the little ones with.

"The stairs..." Emmie looked around, confused. She was sure this was the passage where Jack had pulled faces at her, so where was the staircase?

"Oh!" Emmie jumped as another gasping cry came almost next to her, and Lucy sprang out of her arms and padded away, nosing at a door up ahead, one that was drawn nearly shut. The noise was so sad. Emmie guessed that the child was trying desperately hard not to make a noise, but every so often, they had to gasp for breath, and couldn't help it.

Behind the door were the stairs she had noticed before, only a few steps leading up in a twist to a child's bedroom, lit by a night light just like her own.

Emmie blinked as she came up into the soft light of the candle. She saw Lucy spring on to the bed, and nose forward curiously. And then the crying child sat up and stared.

"What are you doing here?" Jack said, but his voice was shaken and full of tears, and he didn't sound angry, only desperately sad.

"I heard you."

He slumped back on to his pillow, with his back to her. "Go away then. Go and tell everyone you heard me crying, so you can all laugh."

Emmie stood hesitating at the foot of his bed. She had solved the mystery, but she didn't feel proud of herself. It wasn't enough. She sighed. "Can I sit down? Please? This floor's cold."

"S'pose." He glanced at her over his shoulder, but he didn't sit up. Lucy sat down on his feet, and started to wash her ears. Jack looked at them both uncertainly, as if he thought maybe he should kick them off. "You should go back to your own room, if you're cold," he growled.

"What's the matter?"

"Nothing."

"I heard you before, you know. I thought you were a ghost."

He snorted. "There isn't any such thing." It seemed to cheer him up a bit, thinking that she was wrong, and he sat up again, moving his feet very carefully so as not to disturb the cat.

"If there was, it would be here." Emmie shrugged. "This place ought to be full of ghosts, it's so old."

"There is sort of a ghost, in the garden."

Emmie's eyes widened. "Which garden?"

"The one where you were – well. You know." He looked at her shiftily, and gave a damp sniff.

"Where I was crying like you were just now, you mean?"

He nodded, and looked away.

"What sort of ghost?"

"My grandmother." He sounded rather proud of it.

"Have you seen your grandmother's ghost?" Emmie squeaked.

"Not really seen… It's more of a feeling." He reached out cautiously to pat Lucy and then looked up at Emmie. "Do you think I'm making it up?"

"I don't know. What do you mean, a feeling?"

"She died in that garden. A branch broke off the tree while she was sitting on it – just a low one, like a seat. But she was going to have a baby, which was my father. He came early, and she died."

"Oh. . ." Emmie bit her lip. She'd never felt anything – but then, it wasn't her grandmother.

"She came back to the garden."

Emmie watched his face – the clear grey eyes, shining in the candlelight. He didn't look as though he was trying to make fun of her.

"Is she still there?" she asked, whispering.

"My father thinks so. He took my brother and me there when we were only just born, to show us to her." His voice was shaking again, and Emmie saw him rub his eyes. They were shining with tears.

She chewed her bottom lip for a moment, and then edged a little closer, putting her hand close to his on Lucy's back. "When will your brother come on leave?"

"No one knows," Jack said, his voice choked. "He doesn't know either. He sends letters, but they never say very much. He's almost finished his training now. He'll start flying sorties soon – that means attacks against the enemy."

"You must be proud of him then," Emmie suggested cautiously.

Jack only sniffed again. "I have to be, don't I? Everyone says that." He glared at her. "I'd rather he was here. I don't care. Right now in the middle of the night, I don't want to have a brother who's a hero. I just want him to be here. It's easier to be proud of him in the daytime. Now I just keep thinking of his plane getting shot down."

"That won't happen!" Emmie assured him, putting her hand on top of his, but he snatched it away furiously.

"How do you know? You don't know anything about it! Thousands and thousands of things could go wrong. What if he has to bail out?"

Emmie shrugged. She didn't know what that meant either.

He shook his head in frustration. "Uuurrgh! Jump! With his parachute. Do you know what that is?"

"Yes!" Thanks to Arthur and Joey going on and on about flying, she did. "I'm not stupid." She looked at him thoughtfully. "You know, if you told the boys your brother was a pilot, they'd like you more."

He stared at her contemptuously. "Think I care?"

She shrugged again. "It was just a thought. Anyway, I suppose it doesn't matter; aren't you going back to your posh school soon?"

"Not allowed," he growled. "Doctor said I've still got to get better. More."

"You look well enough." Emmie smiled to herself. "Maybe you should spend more time in the garden."

He frowned at her. "What's that supposed to mean?"

Emmie had forgotten for a moment that she wasn't supposed to have read the diaries. She leaned forward to stroke Lucy again while she thought what to say, but Jack flung himself back against the pillows. Lucy glared at him, and dug her claws into the quilt.

"Did my mother tell you all those stupid stories?" Jack growled. "About the magic? It's all nonsense. Magic is just silly. How could a garden make someone better? It's just a bedtime story she used to tell me, that's all."

"She hasn't told me anything! I only meant that fresh air's good for you. Miss Dearlove always says so. But actually, I don't think it is nonsense." Emmie looked up at him, and folded her arms stubbornly. "I believe in the magic. The garden brought me Lucy back."

He laughed scornfully. "No, that was my father."

"I wished for her. Over and over. I dreamed of her in the garden with me, and now it's real. I imagined her sleeping there in the sun, and she does. She did today, while I was weeding around the bulbs coming up. She sat on the ledge round the bottom of the statue, and she had her eyes closed, and the sun shone on her whiskers. It came true."

"David used to play hide and seek with me in that garden," Jack muttered reluctantly. Emmie could see he didn't really want to tell her, but he had to say it to somebody. She just happened to be there. He'd turned his face away from her and it was hard to hear.

"It would be so good for hide and seek," Emmie said, pretending not to notice that there were tears on his face again. "There are so many places to hide. The birds are all in there, in the bushes, even though there's hardly any leaves yet. When it's summer, it'll be the safest place in England. Mr Sowerby said that." She eyed him sideways, and saw that he was still struggling not to cry. She kept on talking. "The robin's looking for a place to build a nest already, did you know? I saw him darting in and out of the ivy, and another robin was with him. I'm sure they were looking for a place for her to lay her eggs. But I'm worried about Lucy. I don't think she really knows how to hunt birds yet, there weren't that many around in our street, but she'll learn. She's watching them already." Emmie looked down at Lucy, stretched smugly on Jack's patchwork quilt. "She loves it here. I don't think she'll ever want to be a London cat again."

Then she stared very hard at Lucy's flicking tail. It wasn't only Lucy. The newspapers in the servants' hall were already full of stories about evacuees being collected by their parents and taken home, because there were no bombs falling on London after all. What if Miss Dearlove and Miss Rose decided that they should go back too? After five months away, Emmie found it hard to imagine being shut up in city streets again.

She bit her lips together, her face twisting as she struggled to hold her own tears in.

"What are *you* crying for?"

"Because I like it here too!" Emmie wailed. "I never meant to." Lucy sat up and nudged against her arm, nibbling at Emmie's wrist with her teeth. She hated it when anyone cried – it made her jumpy and vicious.

"What a stupid thing to cry about." Jack sneered at her, his mouth curling. "Even the cat thinks you should shut up. How can you cry because you're happy?"

"You don't know anything. You don't know how lucky you are," she hissed. "You've got a family, even if you are worried about them. I don't have anyone but Lucy, and I don't belong. You've got everything!"

He looked so surprised that it was almost funny. Emmie eyed him with her head on one side. "Didn't you know we were all orphans? Or just not wanted, anyway. We don't know. None of us knows where we came from."

"It doesn't mean no one wanted you – maybe there was an accident or something," he said uncomfortably.

Emmie shrugged. "Maybe. But to be honest, it's more likely my mother got in the family way when she shouldn't have."

He went red, slowly, all the way to the tips of his ears, and Emmie giggled. She couldn't help it; he was so funny and horrified, and his pale skin went red in waves, like sloshing paint about. "I suppose I shouldn't have said that. It's true, though."

"Aren't you embarrassed about it?" he whispered.

Emmie shrugged. "No. I'm cross with her. Or them – whatever happened. They shouldn't have given me up, even if I wasn't a pretty baby. I wish I had a place that was mine. That's why. . ." She trailed off, and then sighed. "I pretended the garden was mine. No one ever seemed to go in it. It was a place just for me."

He looked sideways at her. "I could help you, with that weeding," he muttered sleepily. "You could show me where the robin's nest is."

"I think it's in the roses, in that dark tangled bit, the corner just along from the bench."

He nodded. "That's a white rose. It's half-wild, but Mother loves it. David showed me a secret tunnel underneath it once, but I got stuck in the thorns; he had to pull me out." He yawned, wriggling down a little more on his pillows. "Did you see the robin fly in there?"

"Again and again," Emmie whispered, watching him struggle to keep his eyes open. His eyelids fluttered, thin and fragile-looking and blue. She could tell he had been ill. "He must have a mate. Perhaps she's sitting in the nest already. Perhaps she'll lay eggs any day soon, deep in the roses. . ."

Chapter Seven

"I can't see anything," Jack complained, shifting grumpily on the painted metal bench. "And I'm cold. Can't we go in?"

"No. Sssshhhh. Any minute now, I bet." Emmie knelt up, peering around them at the tangle of rose stems and ivy in the corner of the garden. That patch was wilder than the rest – Emmie thought that perhaps when Mary and Dickon and Colin had rediscovered the garden, they had left that corner wild for the sake of the birds, and it had stayed that way. "It isn't that cold, anyway. All the snow's gone." To Emmie, the spring sunshine felt delicious, even if wasn't really warm. It made her cheerful. She kept finding unexpected things, first the snowdrops, and now primroses everywhere, in little creamy clusters.

"So? I know it's gone, that doesn't make it summer, you know. The wind's still cold."

Emmie turned back to look at him, suddenly worried. Perhaps it was because he'd been so ill with measles. Maybe it really was too cold for him? She was used to sitting for hours on a freezing fire escape, after all. Even Lucy had preferred to stay inside today. She was curled up by the huge stove, charming Mrs Evans into her feeding her scraps.

"Don't look at me like that," Jack muttered, turning away from her. "I'm not sick. I'd have gone back to school ages ago, if they hadn't evacuated it so far away. And I'm stronger than you. I could beat you in a race."

A flutter of brown feathers caught Emmie's eye, and she reached behind her, grabbing at Jack's arm. "Look!" she whispered, leaning her head fiercely towards the grey rose stems. "Look! I told you."

The robin was perched among the faded stems, his fragile claws planted between the thorns, and some little insect caught in his beak. He eyed the children suspiciously, and Emmie caught her breath. What if they were too close? What if he decided that he and his mate should not make their nest here after all? But he gave them one last stare, and darted further in, so that all they could see of him was a faint dark movement in the coiling branches.

"He's feeding her," Jack said. "They've built the nest, and now he's bringing her food to build up her strength. Or maybe she's even laid the eggs already. I don't know, it might be too early."

Emmie turned round to look at him, wide-eyed. "You know all about birds' nests?"

Jack shrugged. "Only what everybody knows. There are nests all over the gardens."

Emmie sighed. "I didn't know. I thought it was special."

Jack looked uncomfortable. "I still wanted to see. I like him." Then he laughed. "He looked a bit like you just then. Sort of grumpy and suspicious."

"He isn't like that at all!" Emmie cried, and then clapped her hand over her mouth, worrying that she'd frightened the robins. But there was no movement inside the clustered stems. "I know he's shy and strange now, but before he was so friendly. He used to come and watch me when I was exploring. It's just like..." She stopped short. She had been going to say that he was like the robin who'd shown Mary the way into the secret garden. She was still sure that he was one of that long-ago robin's descendants. She had even imagined that the story was passed down among the robins, the same way that Mary had passed the story down to her through the diary. Perhaps they whispered it to their babies in the egg. This robin and his mate would tell their eggs. They could be telling it to them now, this very minute.

Emmie looked round to find Jack rolling his eyes at her. "Joey and Arthur are right, calling you Little Dolly Daydream. What were you going to say? About the robin?"

"Only that I wondered if there had been robins nesting here for always," Emmie said quickly.

Jack looked as though he wasn't sure he believed her, but he didn't say so. "Come on. I have to move, or I'm going to freeze on to this bench."

Emmie got up, gasping as her stiffened knees gave. "Ow. Oh, ow…" She balanced on one leg, shaking her foot.

"You look like a stork." Jack snorted. "A stork that's going to fall over. Come on. Is there anything else new since yesterday?"

They had got into the habit of this now – walking around the garden every day to point out the things that had changed and grown. It was better, having someone to show her discoveries to – even if the someone was Jack, rude and surly and far too boastful. Emmie had never expected to like him, but she almost did.

She strolled along the line of trees, peering for leaf buds. Perhaps they were a little larger than they had been the day before? Jack dashed ahead, sniffing like a spaniel, as though he could catch the scent of spring.

"Oh!" Emmie crouched down, and Jack came racing back to her. "These weren't here yesterday! But they must have been..." She frowned at the mound of heart-shaped emerald leaves clustered around the trunk of the bare apple tree. They seemed too bright for her to have missed them. She leaned closer, intrigued, and caught a wisp of sweetness that wasn't only the fresh scent of growing things. There were flowers buried among the leaves, she saw now. Tiny dark purple flowers that seemed too small to send out so strong a perfume. Emmie sat back, frowning. They smelled oddly familiar.

"Violets." Jack squatted down next to her. "Mm. Now I'm hungry."

"What?"

"Well, the sweets." He sighed at her, exasperated

again. "You must have had them sometime. Or seen them in a sweet shop? Mother likes them. She has them in a little tin, violet pastilles, I think they're called. They taste funny – sort of flowery."

Emmie shrugged. "Never heard of them." Sometimes Jack made her feel as if she didn't know anything. She didn't want to say that she had never been to a sweet shop. "Are they made of these?"

"Yes. And they make scent too. Your Miss Dearlove wears it. It's horrible."

Emmie nodded, a smile lifting one corner of her mouth. That was what the smell was. "It's nicer on the flowers. On Miss Dearlove it smells a bit musty."

Two days later, Emmie found a little tin, sitting on her bed, white, with a pattern of purple flowers painted on, flowers like the ones she had found in the garden. She could see that the tin said Violet on it, but most of the other words she didn't understand. She suspected they might be French. Emmie levered it open with her nails, sniffing as a wave of sugar and flowers poured out. Inside were tiny sweets, richly purple and pressed into the shape of flowers. She slipped one into her mouth, smiling in surprise at the intense sweetness. The sweet stayed in the side of her cheek all through afternoon lessons, until she crunched it as she chased Jack out into the garden. Emmie suspected that the tin might last her for ever.

Emmie followed Jack anxiously along the passage. She could see his white shirt in the dim light, she had her eyes fixed on it. The house was so large, and although she had been all round the gardens, she had never explored much inside at all. "We aren't allowed," she'd told Jack, when he first suggested it.

"I am. It's my house," Jack pointed out, with his lordly air.

"Miss Sowerby said we weren't to."

"You can come if you're with me. And besides, what else are you going to do?" Jack waved at the window – the rain was so heavy that it seemed to be running down the glass in sheets. Lucy was sitting on the windowsill staring out at it disapprovingly. As Jack marched to the door of the schoolroom, she sprang down, and set off after him, waving her tail like a flag.

Emmie looked hesitantly around the room. It *was* Jack's house. She gave up worrying and chased after them down the passage, and then another passage, and another, past suits of armour, and strange dark paintings, and hundreds and hundreds of doors.

"I'm lost," Emmie called anxiously, and Jack turned back to grin at her. "Where are we going, anyway? I don't have any idea how to get back." Then she bit her lip worriedly, hoping she wasn't giving him ideas of running off and leaving her behind. Nobody would find her for years. She'd *die*, and by the time anyone thought to look for her she'd just be a pile of bones. Emmie shuddered. Was that what was in all those old wooden chests they kept walking past?

"I don't either," Jack admitted cheerfully. "But I always get back in the end. No one really uses this bit of the house, they haven't for years and years. Even before Mother had to shut bits up because of the war. It's like being explorers."

"You don't know where you're going?" Emmie hissed.

"No. I was going to show you the elephants, but I thought we'd get to them about three corners ago, and we haven't."

"Elephants?" Emmie was momentarily distracted from being furious with him.

"Carved ivory ones – there are ninety-six of them, I counted. Some of them are only as big as my thumbnail. They live in a cabinet in a room at this end of the house *somewhere*."

"Don't you mind being lost?" Emmie asked him. He didn't seem to be worried at all.

Jack shrugged. "I'll work out where we are eventually. And if I don't, someone will always come and find me."

Emmie supposed that actually, someone would come and find her too. She just wasn't quite as sure of it as he was.

Jack looked around at the heavy wooden doors, and then marched over to open one. Emmie had thought they might all be locked, but the door opened easily, with only a faint wheezing creak.

"I wonder when anyone last came in here," Jack murmured, looking round the door. "It smells of dust." He put his hands in his pockets and strolled in, but Emmie thought perhaps he was only pretending not to care. The empty stillness of the room was daunting.

The rain made the room dimly grey, so that the furniture seemed to loom at them out of the shadows. There was a huge bed up against the wall, carved from black wood, and draped with heavy red velvet curtains. Emmie couldn't imagine sleeping in it, swathed in dark, dusty stuff. It would be impossible to breathe.

Lucy jumped up on to the gilt-embroidered coverlet and sneezed as a little cloud of dust puffed up under her paws.

Emmie followed her into the room, looking around cautiously. She almost expected the room's owner to appear, and tell them to get out. It did seem like a room that had belonged to someone, once. There were ornaments on the mantelpiece, and a dressing table over by the window, with more red velvet for a skirt. The mirror was dark with greenish spots. Emmie turned away from it suddenly, afraid that she might see another face behind her own.

The walls were covered in tapestries, like the ones in Emmie's own room, but these hangings made a garden. Stiff, formal flowers twined all over them, and birds perched here and there. Emmie walked around the room examining them, and trying to see what the flowers were.

"There's a rabbit!" The little creature was hunched nervously in one corner under a tree covered in fruit. She turned to Jack, shaking her head. "Are all the rooms like this?" she murmured.

Jack nodded. "Mostly. I haven't explored all of them, though. It's not as much fun on your own. David used to make trails," he added, his eyes widening as though he'd forgotten. "He had a ball of string, so we could follow it back."

Emmie rolled her eyes. "And you didn't think to bring one? I must say, your brother sounds a lot cleverer than you."

"He's better at everything than me." Jack's voice was small, and he didn't look at her, just went on leaning on the windowsill, gazing down at the gardens in the rain. "We're not as far round as I thought we were. I can see the kitchen gardens, look."

"I didn't mean it," Emmie said guiltily. "I mean, of course he's better at things than you. He's years older, isn't he?"

"Eight," Jack agreed. "But he used to let me follow him around when he was home in the holidays. He liked it. Dad used to say it was as if David had a puppy." He frowned suddenly, and pulled away from the window. "I *have* been in this room before, I'd forgotten. It was years and years ago." He plunged across the room to a huge wardrobe standing in the corner furthest from the window, and flung the doors open. "I thought so." Emmie peered over his shoulder. The bottom of the wardrobe was piled with round boxes, patterned and striped in faded colours, and fastened with ribbon. Jack fought with a bow, and then lifted off the lid from the topmost box, grinning. "Can you imagine wearing this?" He pulled out a hat that was so huge it looked more like a cake, or a meringue. Mrs Evans and Mrs Martin had been trying to find ideas to get round rationing by looking at old recipe books, but mostly it had just made them feel worse. Emmie had seen a whole page with drawings of elaborate desserts that looked like this hat. It was swathed in puffs of net, dotted with little silk flowers, and ribbon rosettes. Jack reached out and perched it on Emmie's head, yanking it down around her ears and making her squeak. It was surprisingly heavy.

Jack pushed her over towards the spotted mirror on the dressing table, and Emmie let him. The hat might have belonged to Mary, or perhaps to Jack's grandmother who haunted the garden. She wanted to see it. There were no such things as ghosts, she told herself.

There was so much hat that she could hardly see anything of herself underneath it. She was no more than a small, freckled nose and a pointed chin, sticking out under a pile of flowered net. Lucy sprang on to the dressing table and peered up at her worriedly.

"It's all right," Emmie murmured. "I know it looks

like it's eating me, but it isn't. This hat is the silliest thing I've ever seen... Actually, no." She had turned round, and caught Jack in an absurdly tall grey top hat that was falling down round his ears. "That is." She pressed her hand across her mouth, giggling and sneezing in the drifts of dust as Jack let go of the hat, and it sank slowly over his eyebrows.

"Get it off me!"

"I think you look better like that," Emmie told him, straight-faced, as she pulled the top hat off.

"Just watch it, or I really will leave you here..." Jack told her, as they packed the hats away. Then he grabbed her hand. "Come on. I want to find those elephants."

Emmie was hidden, stretched out flat in the damp grass under one of the lilac bushes. It had dark pinkish-purple flowers, great fat clusters of them, and the scent was so sweet that Emmie wanted to drink it.

She could hear Jack tiptoeing around, looking for her. He thought he was being so clever, but she knew exactly where he was. The only thing that might give her away would be if Lucy decided to come and join in. The cat didn't understand hide and seek; if she decided to curl up under the lilac with Emmie, she'd purr and purr, and march around finding the best place to sit. Lucy was sleeping in the sun on the edge of the statue, though. At least, Emmie thought she was. She rolled over a little, peering out past the fringe of long grass. There was still a puddle of black fur slopped languorously over the edge of the stone plinth. Lucy looked like she was melting.

The garden was so still in the early summer heat, with only Jack's footsteps breaking the silence. It was as if the year was making up for the harsh winter, trying to fill everyone with sunlight. Making up for the bad news too. The newspapers seemed to get worse every day. The Germans had invaded Holland and Belgium, and now they had poured into France. There was a British army in France too, the British Expeditionary Force, but it was a lot smaller than the wave of German soldiers, and not properly prepared to fight. It was more of a gesture to show good faith to the French, Jack said. His mother had left a letter from Lieutenant Craven lying around, and Jack had read it. Emmie could tell when he was quoting his father; his voice went slower, and deeper, and there were worried lines above his nose.

Jack lurched from mad games, where he wanted

Emmie to chase him all over the house, or he planned to walk along the top of the kitchen garden wall without falling off, or launch Lucy in his toy sailing boat across the pond, to moments of utter misery. He was anxious about his father, whose ship was guarding convoys on their way to Norway, and even more worried about his brother David, who had been based in France flying a Hurricane to support the British Expeditionary Force.

Now all the planes had been pulled out of France to airbases on the coast, where they had to fly over the Channel to give cover to the army instead. It made the war seem so much closer – that there were only twenty-one miles of sea to keep the Germans away.

The staff in the servants' hall had taken to sitting over the newspapers in the evenings, shaking their heads – the British Expeditionary Force hadn't enough tanks or heavy guns to stand up to the German army. Charlie Barker, one of the under-gardeners, had gone off to enlist back in September, and had been sent to France with the Green Howards, one of the Yorkshire regiments. He'd written to Mr Sowerby that hardly any of his battalion had pistols.

"Not even compasses," Mr Sowerby had snarled, folding the letter with sharp, jerky movements of his hands, and crumpling it as he stuffed it into his pocket. "All to do again, jus' like before. How're the poor sods meant t' find their way back home? Runnin' like rabbits."

Emmie had never seen him so angry – for a few minutes, he was the same distant, growling figure she had first met, so many months before. Remembering, she edged back further under the lilac bush, and shivered a little in the chill of the shadow.

The green door in the wall banged open, and Emmie flinched, scraping her knees on the dry twigs. The quiet, bee-humming afternoon was broken as a figure blundered into the garden.

"Jack! Are you there? Jack! Oh, please. . ."

Emmie heard him turn, his sandals hissing on the dry grass. He was still playing hide and seek; he waited for a moment, caught in the game. Then something made him run. He hurled himself at his mother.

It was the colour of the paper. Emmie saw it a few seconds after Jack did. Even from the shadows under the lilac bush, she knew what it was. A telegram. Everyone knew what that colour of paper meant. Mrs Martin the cook had received a telegram to tell her that her son had been injured while he was fighting in the army in Norway, and she had refused to open the yellow envelope. She was quite certain that the message was to tell her that Will was dead. She had sat holding it, and staring at it, and turning it over in her hands. Eventually Mrs Evans had sent Joey, telling him to fetch Mrs Craven so she could open the envelope for the cook. Mrs Evans had been so relieved that Will was only wounded that she had hugged everyone in the kitchen, and used all the sugar ration to make cocoa.

"Is it David?" Jack was clinging on to his mother's arm. Emmie wriggled further back under the lilac bush. She shouldn't be here. This was secret – too much of a secret even to fit into the garden. She tried to stuff her fingers into her ears, but she couldn't make herself not hear.

"No." Mrs Craven sat down suddenly on the grass, pulling Jack with her, half on to her lap. "No, darling. It's Dad."

Miss Sowerby told them the news properly at supper time. She slipped into the servants' hall looking thinner, and round-shouldered, as though suddenly she wasn't young any more. There were tears seeping through the smiling creases around her eyes.

She had known Lieutenant Craven since they were both children, since she was a clumsy little servant girl, too countrified really, to work in such a smart house. She had watched over him when he was a bad-tempered, sickly child who wore out his nurse. He had screamed and shouted at her in the middle of the night. And then he had grown up, when everyone had been so sure he never would.

"I never thought," she murmured, dropping into a chair next to Mrs Martin. "After everythin' that happened – there was always a spark of summat in him. They called it Magic, the children, when they were small. Even with the war like it is, I never thought..."

"What happened?" Arthur whispered, his eyes round. They had known he was dead – not from Emmie, they had seen Mrs Craven's face as she ran calling through the gardens. She and Jack had stumbled together back into the house, and shut themselves away in Lieutenant Craven's study.

"Is it certain?" Emmie asked, at the same time. "It couldn't be a mistake?"

Miss Sowerby reached out to stroke her cheek. "I can't see it bein' wrong, Emmie. The telegram had his name, his number an' all. It happened a week ago. There's a letter to follow, they said. It was th' Admiralty sent the telegram, they must know."

"A week? He was at Dunkirk, then?" Joey leaned forward eagerly. "We thought that! When it came on the radio, we wondered if Lieutenant Craven might be there." He was smiling excitedly – it *had* been exciting, hearing it. Emmie and Ruby had hugged each other, and Ruby had done a little dance around the kitchen. All those little ships, sailing off to France to rescue the brave soldiers, and bring them home. Some of them had been fishing boats, the man on the radio had said. Some of them were the sort of boats that took people on outings at the seaside. Britain had called, and the men in those boats had answered, everyone said. The story had been so dramatic that the rescue felt almost like a victory, not the crushing defeat it really was.

Joey ducked his head, his cheeks pink, suddenly remembering. "Sorry," he whispered.

Miss Sowerby only smiled at him, the tears slowly spreading down her cheeks.

"He was good at rescuing things," Emmie whispered. "If he'd go to all that trouble for Lucy, he'd make them pick up those poor soldiers from the water. That will be what happened. They were rescuing the soldiers."

Joey nodded. "Maybe a U-boat..." But then he snapped his mouth shut again, as Emmie and Miss Dearlove and Miss Rose all turned on him with a fierce glare. Miss Sowerby leaned forward, pressing her hands over her face, and Joey hunched down, trying to make himself look small.

"It's not a *story*," Emmie hissed, and Joey nodded, just a little apologetic twitch of his head. It was hard not to talk about it. He wanted to know. The news had caught everyone's imagination.

So many of the rooms were closed up and covered in dust sheets now that Mrs Craven had taken to sitting downstairs in the kitchen or the servants' hall sometimes, especially to listen to the evening news. She said it was too lonely, hearing it upstairs on her own. But she didn't come down that evening, and neither did Jack.

Jack didn't appear at lessons the next day either. Emmie watched the door, hoping for him to slip in. She didn't know what she could say to him, but she hated the thought that he was hidden away again, desperate. Even more desperate now than he had been the night she went to find him in the dark.

"I expect Jack needs to be with his mother now," Miss Rose murmured. "We must leave them alone." She was looking at Emmie as she said it, and Emmie nodded, though inside she wanted to argue. What if Jack wanted someone else to talk to? Or needed someone, even if he didn't want them very much. She wouldn't mind if he yelled at her again... Emmie leaned on her hand, and stabbed her pencil at the page. Well. She would mind. But she wouldn't yell back, she promised herself.

He still has a mother... something whispered inside her. *You don't have anyone.*

"But I never did have," she murmured to herself. "It isn't the same." Then she looked across at Arthur expecting him to be smirking at her for talking to herself. But he was drawing tiny ships in the margins of his sums, and Joey was gazing into the distance across the room. For once, it could have been Emmie that teased them for daydreaming, but all she did was kick Joey gently under the table, and nod sideways. Miss Dearlove was watching.

Emmie bolted her lunch down, eager to get out into the gardens, away from the brooding sadness of the house. The roses were coming out. She hadn't believed that there could be more flowers in the secret garden than when she had first seen it in September, but the buds were everywhere, unfurling, lines of pink and white and blazing red bursting through the green. There were more every day. She sped up as she ran down the paved walk by the gardens – there was a rose that climbed around the statue where Lucy liked to sleep, an early-flowering one that she had never seen open. Jack had told her that it was striped, dark red with white, and Emmie could see it in her head, like the stiff silk dress of the little girl in the painting that hung in their schoolroom. Even Jack didn't know who she was, but she made Emmie laugh. She looked so cross. Her parents couldn't have been pleased with the portrait, Emmie thought. The poor painter must have tried to make her smile, or at least look grand and proud. But the girl's mouth was dragged into a determined line, and her eyes were snapping. She had wanted to be outside, Emmie was sure. Perhaps she had wanted to run about in the garden and stroke the petals of the striped roses, instead of being laced into that tight dress and made to stand still. Even the little dog in her arms was gazing wistfully out of the side of the frame – it wanted to dash about over the grass too.

Emmie twisted the brass handle under the ivy, and eased the door open, slipping through and looking eagerly over at the statue. She darted across the lawn to see if the striped flowers had opened yet, but then a fluttering of pink caught her eye, and she spun round.

Mrs Craven was lying on the grass under the great tree, her pink cotton dress the same colour as the rose petals scattered around her. Fistfuls of them. Emmie stared at them, not understanding. Mr Sowerby always made sure that the bush just next to the tree was watered, and carefully trimmed. The flowers had hardly opened, and now the bush was almost bare, a few buds limply trailing from the branches.

Mrs Craven put one hand up to shield her eyes from the sun, and squinted at Emmie as if she wasn't sure who this was in her garden. Her hand was scratched – there was a thin trickle of dark blood running down on to her wrist.

"You tore all the flowers off," Emmie whispered, shocked. "What did you do that for?"

Mrs Craven didn't say anything – she just went on staring at Emmie as though she were a stranger.

Emmie stepped back, suddenly frightened. Mrs

Craven's face was so pale, her eyes looked almost black.

"Come away, lass." Mr Sowerby caught her arm, and Emmie gasped – she hadn't even heard him limping up behind her. "She needs us gone."

"But the roses. . ." Emmie whispered.

"Do as tha'rt told!" He pulled at her arm sharply, and Emmie cried out – he'd hurt her, even though she could see that he hadn't meant to. He hustled her back out of the green door and on to the path. "I'm sorry, Emmie. Mrs Craven needs th' garden now, doesn't tha' see it? Tha' just let her be. Did I hurt thee?"

"Yes." Emmie sniffed, rubbing her wrist. "A lot. When can I go and look at the roses?"

He shook his head, and then rubbed a hand wearily across his reddened eyes. His scars looked darker. "No. Tha' can't. Didn't tha' listen? It's her place, hers and his, their secret. Leave her alone. Stay out."

Emmie gazed at him, dumbfounded, and then shook her head. "No! I can't – you don't mean it."

But he hardly seemed to be hearing her. He turned away and began to hobble up the path, back to the kitchen gardens.

"But who's going to look after the garden?" Emmie wailed. She ran after him, pulling at his jacket. "I help, don't I? Please? You can't make me stay away."

"I'll do it," he growled. "Get away with thee, child. Buzzing about like a wasp, th'art."

Emmie dropped back, staring after him with her eyes stinging. Even when she'd first arrived, he'd never spoken to her like that. It almost sounded as if he hated her. Emmie watched him until he limped into one of the kitchen gardens, and then she walked back to the door under the ivy. She wanted to sneak back in and she didn't think Mrs Craven was in a state to notice. But then the brass doorknob under her hand was cold – it seemed to have lost some of its worn silken feel, that inviting golden softness that always tempted her in. Even in the hot June sunshine, the cold metal bit into her fingers, and Emmie stepped back.

She wasn't wanted.

Emmie lay on the warm stone slabs around the pool, with Lucy sitting next to her. Both of them were staring at the fish, and occasionally Lucy would put out a hopeful paw, and then draw it back again. She wanted the little golden things so much, and she spent hours watching them, but she was afraid of the water.

"What if I can never go back?" Emmie whispered to her. "What if he meant for always?" She sat up, drawing her knees up under her chin, and closed her eyes, trying to see the garden in her head. But there was too much of it, too much to see and smell and touch. Even when she told it to herself as a story, only a hint of the magic came through. She needed to step through the door.

"I should have taken you with me," she muttered, running her hand over Lucy's sun-warmed fur. "No one ever tells you where to go." She looked over her shoulder at the long flower bed, blazing with pink lilies, and hissed through her teeth. The heat was bringing them all on, and they were opening out like great cups – but it wasn't the same. "I *know* that rose would be out. I could go back – Mrs Craven must have gone by now. And I don't think she'd mind if I was there, anyway. She knows I love the garden. Emmie told Lieutenant Craven how helpful I was." Emmie rocked back and forth gently, hugging her knees. "I could go back," she whispered again. But she didn't get up. She could – but she wouldn't.

17th June 1910

Even the walls are covered now – tiny creeping plants have seeded themselves in the cracks between the bricks, and smothered them in flowers. White daisies, with each petal dipped in pink, and tiny little yellow flowers that look like specks of gold. One of the statues has a great clump of violet-blue campanula trailing out of the wall behind her; it's grown down all over her shoulders like a cape of little bells.

There are so many columbines I could gather armfuls and fill a vase in each room of the house, if it wasn't such a pity to pick them. They must be named after the dancing girl in the stories, I'm sure; they dance and shake their frilly petals as the wind blows through them. Today I lay down next to the tallest purple delphiniums, the ones that are almost as tall as me, and stared up at the sky. I made patterns out of the clouds. Colin said I looked quite mad, and even Dickon was trying not to smile, but I don't care.

Emmie padded silently through the night-dark passages and up the steps to Jack's room. She had been dreaming about the garden, Mary's garden. She had found the pages in the diary for the summer, all those years ago. She could see the garden as she read – the words made it even harder not to be there. But she couldn't stop.

Then in her dream she had got in there again at last – but the garden had kept changing, stretching out into tunnels of dark shadow. Emmie ran and ran to reach the bright sunlight and the roses, but could never escape the clinging greyness of the tunnel. She had woken up gasping, choking, to find Lucy stretched across her chest weighing her down – and grumpy when she tried to move.

Too scared to go back to sleep, in case she slipped back into the shadows again, Emmie got out of bed. She would go and find Jack, she decided. Maybe he wouldn't want to talk to her, but at least she could try. Lucy stood up and stared at her, and then clambered quickly into the warm spot that Emmie had left in the bed, and curled up again.

The house was silent, and when she peered through the heavy curtains in the passageway outside Jack's room the night was black. It must be late – the middle of the night. Emmie paused at the top of the steps, chewing her lip and peering into the darkness of the room. He was probably fast asleep. It was stupid to have come.

"What are you doing?"

Emmie nearly shrieked. Jack wasn't in bed – he was curled up on the wide stone windowsill, glaring at her. The moonlight glimmered on the side of his face. He looked cold, and miserable.

"Why aren't you in bed?" she snapped, surprised into sharpness. She'd forgotten that his father had died, and that she'd come all prepared to be nice to him.

"Why aren't you?"

Emmie shrugged. "I dreamt – something bad. I thought I'd come and see you. To see if you were all right..." She ducked her head, embarrassed. It sounded so stupid. How could he be?

"I am. Now go away."

Emmie swallowed down another sharp answer. "Do I have to?" she asked, her voice almost pleading. "I don't want to dream it again. Can't I stay here for a little bit?"

"No."

"You don't have to be so mean."

"Yes, I do." Jack spat out each word, and Emmie suddenly recognized the way he was talking. He was all buttoned up. Even his mouth was tidy, the lips pressed together. His hands were folded in his lap, the knuckles white. If he let himself go, he was going to scream.

"It might be better if. . ."

"What?"

Emmie shook her head. "Nothing. I'll go then. Shall I?"

"Yes. Go away."

Emmie began to shuffle away towards the steps, still looking at him, hoping that he'd change his mind. He watched her go – she could see the sharp glitter of his eyes in the light from the window. As she reach the top of the steps, Emmie was almost sure she saw him lean forward – did he reach out one hand, to snatch her back? But he said nothing. What would he do if she ran back, and hugged him, and curled up next to him on the windowsill? Probably push her off. Or cry. She wasn't sure which would be worse.

"Night," she murmured.

"Go away."

Chapter Eight

Working in the kitchen garden, Emmie could smell the roses. The scent wafted over the high wall, sweet and tempting. Emmie sighed. She could go in – the door wasn't locked, and she was almost sure that Mrs Craven was in the house. After the first few days of quiet strangeness, she had gone back to her old self, or seemed to have done. She smiled at the children when she passed them. She went back to her volunteer work at the convalescent home in Thwaite, and she talked to everyone the way she always had.

But she didn't let anyone else back into the garden. Emmie saw her going in there almost every afternoon. She had gloves on, and tools with her, sometimes she was even wheeling a barrow. Mr Sowerby worked there too, but in the afternoons, he left her to be in the garden alone. Emmie wondered why Mrs Craven never cried – she didn't listen, exactly, but it was like the roses, she was only just across the wall, she couldn't help hearing. Mrs Craven didn't cry. Occasionally she sang, very quietly, and Emmie wasn't quite sure of the song. A nursery rhyme, she thought.

Now she put out a hand, and stroked the crumbling brick of the wall. It was comforting to be so close. She knew that the garden was still there, quiet and mysterious. But it made it so hard to stay away, knowing that she could just run along the path, and sneak behind the ivy. She had the strangest feeling that the garden was lonely without her – that it needed her and Jack, playing hide and seek, or tag, or stretched out in the grass watching the two robins fussing around their nest.

She had seen the male robin several times that afternoon, darting importantly over the wall, trailing worms almost as long as he was. The robins' first brood had hatched out weeks before, and flown the nest, but Jack had told her that there might be two lots of eggs, or even three. The robin was feeding his wife and his second clutch of children now – they had hatched just days before that afternoon of hide and seek. Now they must be fully feathered, almost as big as their parents. It was no wonder the robin looked harassed. Emmie watched him longingly, wishing she could swoop into the secret garden as easily as he could.

Jack still hadn't spoken to her since she'd gone to his room a week before. He hadn't come back to lessons, and Miss Rose hadn't said anything about it to his mother. Emmie didn't know what he was doing – she saw him in the distance occasionally, vanishing round the corner of a passageway, or slipping behind a door. She'd tried running after him, but he always seemed to be just too far ahead. He knew the house well enough to disappear behind a tapestry, or slide behind a suit of armour, so that she'd never find him. He was determined to be left alone.

Emmie turned round, and leaned against the wall, closing her eyes, and feeling the sun-warmed brick against her back. She could see leaves dancing behind her eyelids, glowing in the sun, and splashed with bright petals. She ached with longing, deep inside. It hurt to be so close.

Emmie's breath caught in a little surprised noise. She hadn't heard Lucy padding along the flagged path towards her. The cat wove lovingly around Emmie's boots, purring. Emmie picked her up, and she dug her claws in and out of the sleeve of Emmie's cardigan, her eyes closed to blissful slits. Then she abruptly wriggled on to Emmie's shoulder, and sprang up on to the top of the wall. She scrabbled a little as she reached the top, and then glared triumphantly down at Emmie.

"Oh, Lucy. . ." Emmie sighed. "Not you too. It isn't fair."

The black cat padded smugly along the top of the wall for a few steps, and then stopped, her tail twitching slowly from side to side, and her green gaze fixed.

Emmie watched her, suddenly anxious. What had she seen? It was probably just a butterfly. Lucy loved to chase them, sitting up on her haunches and batting at them with her long black paws. "Don't eat it. . ." Emmie whispered. She had eaten one yesterday, such a pretty one – the soft blue wings had looked so strange sticking out of Lucy's furry mouth. And the cat hadn't even liked it much, she'd spat most of it back out.

"Oh no…" Emmie stepped back and stretched up on tiptoe, trying to see over the wall, to see what Lucy was seeing. But the wall was too high – she could only glimpse the tops of the trees. "No, you can't…"

Lucy wasn't listening to her. She was creeping along the top of the wall, her tail swishing.

The robin was perched in the tree on the other side of the wall. He was pecking at the bark – it looked like there was an insect creeping about in the tiny cracks. He dragged it out triumphantly, and fluttered away – and Lucy leaped down after him, on the other side of the wall.

"Lucy!" Emmie hissed. "Lucy, come back! You mustn't! You can't chase him, he's got babies…" Then she grimaced to herself. Lucy wasn't stupid. She would sneak across the grass, following the robin to the nest, and she would see that there were more of these soft, delicious, fluttery things. With the last clutch, Jack and Emmie had shooed her away – Jack had even found several beetles one morning, and put them down in a line in front of Lucy as a distraction. But there was no one to watch out for the robins now.

The little cat was all on her own in the garden, hunting.

"She'll eat them," Emmie moaned, scratching at the wall with her fingers, as if she could climb it too. "Lucy, come back…"

It was no good. She whirled round, and raced through the rows of beans and tomatoes towards the path, and the ivy, and the door to the garden.

Even knowing that it wasn't allowed, this time the brass handle didn't feel cold. The metal was warm and welcoming and buttery-soft under her fingers. She twisted it eagerly, so eagerly she almost fell into the garden. As she dashed out on to the grass, searching anxiously for Lucy, she could feel something tight inside her easing away. The rustling, twittering quiet seemed to seep in under her skin.

Lucy was stalking across the grass towards the tangled corner where so many birds had nested. She seemed to consider each paw before she placed it down, and her shoulders were a little hunched, ready to spring.

Emmie ran after her, and Lucy glanced round, startled by the heavy footsteps.

"No! Shoo!" Emmie flapped her hands at the cat, and Lucy dodged her irritably, still intent on her hunting.

Then the robin fluttered out of the dense thicket with a sharp, stuttering trill, and Lucy turned away, sitting down in the grass as if she'd never meant anything. She even swiped one paw across her muzzle, licking at it, and then looking at Emmie sideways, as if to say she'd only been washing. Nothing else.

Emmie smiled lovingly at her. She knew that Lucy would be straight back to the robin's nest as soon as she thought Emmie wasn't looking. Perhaps she should warn Mr Sowerby? But he was still hardly talking to anyone – he didn't do much more than growl instructions when she asked him for garden jobs. Though he had patted her shoulder the day before, when she'd shown him the trug full of peas that she had picked. He hadn't said anything, but she was almost sure that he was sorry he'd shouted at her – or at least *regretful*. He just couldn't bring himself to tell her so.

She crouched down, scooping Lucy into her arms. They would go and watch the fish in the lily pond, she knew Lucy couldn't catch those. She sighed, and looked round at the roses, pouring down the walls in blazing fountains of pink and red and white – she couldn't stay. She knew it. The longer she stayed now, the harder it would be to tear herself away.

As she walked back across the lawn, she heard the footsteps, quick and light – someone in the kitchen garden? Emmie whirled round, scanning the trees. She had played hide and seek in here so many times – why couldn't she see anywhere to hide now? The handle was turning, she could hear that funny little squeak it made. Emmie stepped back, and another step, and another, and the door opened.

Mrs Craven came in with a basket, and secateurs in her hand. She had a straw hat on, shading her eyes, and Emmie was standing so frozen-still that at first she didn't notice the girl. Mrs Craven almost walked into her, and then stopped short, gasping and white-faced, as though she were truly frightened.

That was what Lieutenant Craven's death had done to her, Emmie realized, full of guilt. It was as if her skin had been stripped away. When that piece of yellow paper had ripped her life apart, she had lost all her protection, all her padding. Now everything hurt.

Mrs Craven simply stared at her, and Emmie couldn't think what to say. She had missed the garden so much while she was exiled from it that she could understand how much Jack's mother needed to be there. She needed that calm sense of everything growing and flowering and just going on. Looking at her now, Emmie almost agreed that the garden should be hers – almost.

"I'm sorry." Her voice was a squeak of nerves, and Lucy hissed crossly, suddenly clutched too tight.

Mrs Craven shook her head. Either she simply couldn't bring herself to speak, she was too angry, or she was saying it didn't matter. Emmie couldn't tell.

"It was because of Lucy, I know I'm not supposed to be here, I stayed away even though I didn't want to. Really, I did! Please don't be upset. . ." Her voice trailed away. What a stupid thing to say.

The green door crashed open again, and Mr Sowerby lurched through it, too fast and angry to balance himself properly. He almost fell, and Mrs Craven grabbed his arm.

"What did I tell thee?" he roared at Emmie, and Lucy twisted and shot out of Emmie's arms, her ears flat against her narrow skull. She stalked away behind a stand of lilies, and watched them all resentfully. "Stay away, I said!"

"I did!" Emmie yelled back, suddenly angry. "I

did, for days and days! Even when I could have gone in without anyone seeing me, I stayed away."

"Don't shout at her," Mrs Craven murmured, but the gardener was too angry to listen.

"So what are tha' doing here, then? Ungrateful, disobedient wench that th'art!"

"I'm not ungrateful!" Emmie screamed, clenching her fists. "I love it! How can you say I'm ungrateful? You don't know how I feel inside! You tore me out of my place!" She glared at him, and then at Mrs Craven, breathing fast, and trying to think what she had meant. The words had come into her mouth without her thinking them first. "Yes. You did, twice. You dragged us all here, and I suppose that's fair because none of us liked the Home much and we had to be evacuated somewhere, so why not here? But it was different from everything, and I hated it, and I didn't have Lucy. It was only the garden that made it almost all right. Then I loved it, and I shouldn't have done. And you tore me away again."

Mrs Craven was staring at her still, but the white, set look had changed to a sort of puzzled fascination. As if she were trying to recognize something.

"She puts me in mind of thee," Mr Sowerby muttered to her, rubbing one hand over the scarred side of his face. "A long time ago. Before all this." He passed his hand over his face again, as if he could rub the scars away. "Mean-tempered."

"I'm not..." Emmie said, her voice quivering. It hurt more because it was almost true – she *had* been. She was still, sometimes. But not like she had been before. Was she? Wasn't she better? The old Emmie would never have fussed over Ruby and her fish – or made such an effort to comfort Jack.

"I was mean-tempered because I was lonely, even if I didn't know it," Mrs Craven broke in quietly. "Emmie was lonely too. Colin – Lieutenant Craven, I mean... He did something special, bringing your little cat back to you."

Emmie eyed her worriedly, hoping that she wasn't about to cry. Her voice had shaken slightly as she spoke about him.

"And I've seen you with Jack – considering how angry he was to have his home invaded by strangers, you must have put aside some of the meanness, at least. At any rate, there's been something..."

"It was the garden." Emmie twisted her hands over, feeling uncomfortable with this praise. "But I haven't seen Jack properly since ... since his father... I did try. He didn't want to talk to me."

"He doesn't want to talk to anyone," his mother murmured. "I don't think he can yet."

Emmie nodded, and then her eyes widened. She turned and darted across the grass, grabbing at Lucy. The black cat had slunk through the lilies while they were talking, making another stealthy attack on the robins' nest. She retreated behind the statue, sulking.

"I think I'll have to shut her indoors," Emmie said worriedly. "She'll hate it. She was never an indoor cat. She even went out in the snow, and she hated it, but she just couldn't stay inside all the time. I don't know how to stop her. She never really noticed the first clutch hatching, she was too busy watching me and Jack, but now she knows they're there."

Mr Sowerby frowned at her, drawing his one eyebrow down. "Was that why tha' came in here? To stop th' little cat?"

Emmie nodded. "She was in the kitchen garden with me, and she saw the robin go over the wall. She followed him, and I could see it in her eyes, she was so excited. All he could think about was worms, and getting them to his babies. I don't think birds are clever enough to understand they're being hunted –

or not to do anything about it, anyway. They haven't a hope."

"And that was the first time you've been in the garden since Mr Sowerby told you to leave me in peace?" Mrs Craven asked slowly, as if she was trying to understand.

"Yes." Emmie folded her arms and glared. "I did what he said. I thought about not doing it though. I almost went in, a few times."

Mrs Craven actually laughed. A short chuckle, nothing more, but Mr Sowerby looked over at her in relieved surprise. "I stole this garden, Emmie, did you know? It was locked up; no one was supposed to go in it. I can't really complain if you do the same, can I?"

"You stole the garden?" Emmie stared at her, and shook her head, not understanding. There was a hole in the story, and she couldn't quite draw it all back together. "You?" she murmured. "It was you? The girl who found the key? It was your secret garden?" *Before it was mine,* she wanted to say. "Then – you're Mary Lennox?"

Mrs Craven – *Mary* Craven – smiled at her and nodded. "Did Miss Sowerby tell you the story?"

Now would be the time to confess about the

diaries, but Emmie wasn't sure what to say. She was still trying to piece everything together, to fill in the hole. The angry little girl from the diary – Emmie had never been able to think of her grown up, but of course she would be. She had stayed at Misselthwaite.

Emmie took in a sharp breath, and caught Mrs Craven's sleeve. "Colin! You said that it was Colin who brought Lucy back to me. You meant Lieutenant Craven. He was Colin. . ." Emmie's voice faltered away, and she felt her eyes sting. It couldn't be right. Colin was the boy the garden had brought back to life. Surely the magic hadn't healed him for this? Just to die?

Mary pressed one hand over her eyes for a moment, and then nodded at Emmie. "He said he was going to live for ever," she murmured. "We grew out of believing that the garden was full of magic, of course. But I think I still believed that he would. . ."

"It were a cruel waste," Mr Sowerby muttered. "Sit down, Miss Mary." He took her arm, and limped across to one of the stone benches, murmuring to her as if she were a wounded bird.

Emmie watched them, fascinated. Mary. And Dickon. Dickon Sowerby – Mary had even mentioned the name in her diary. The animal-charmer. She felt as though she should have realized before. But how could she have seen the strong, cheerful boy that everyone on the moor had loved in this growling man?

"I shouldn't have shut you out of the garden," Mary said, beckoning to her. "I'm sorry, Emmie, I didn't know." She took Emmie by the hand, pulling her gently to sit on the bench. Then she cupped her hand around Emmie's cheek and studied her face. "Look at you. The magic *was* still there. I should have seen that."

"So … I can come back?" Emmie whispered hopefully, looking up at her.

Dickon grunted. "If tha'rt here, tha' can work. There's weeds among th' lilies. And watch that little beggar of a cat." But he patted her shoulder, and then gripped it, tight, and she knew that he meant it to be sorry.

"That robin Lucy was chasing must be the great-great-grandson of my robin," Mary said, looking dreamily around the garden. "He was so proud of himself, and his beautiful red feathers. He was my first friend here. The first person I actually *wanted* to like me."

Emmie glanced at her in surprise, recognizing the idea. "For me that was Lucy." Then she looked properly at Mary, seeing the soft, remembering look in her eyes. Mary had almost forgotten that she was there. "I'd better go. Miss Rose said about keeping an eye on Ruby..." Emmie murmured. She got up, and backed away slowly, chirruping to Lucy, who padded ungraciously from behind the statue of the foolish-looking girl.

At the door, Emmie turned to look back. Dickon was crouched close by the robins' nest, watching, and Mary was standing on the grass by the rose tree that she had destroyed. She and Colin and Dickon had planted it together, so long ago. There were a few flowers on it, the buds that she had left behind now opened out. Emmie flinched for a second as Mary reached out to one of the pink-tinged flowers, thinking that she meant to tear it off. But all she did was run her fingers over the petals, and she was almost smiling.

Looking after Ruby had been made up as an excuse on the spot, but Emmie thought she might as well go and see if Ruby was by the lily pond. The fish would distract Lucy from robins. But as she hurried

196

down the steps, she realized that the hunched up figure by the water was Jack, not Ruby.

He sprang up at the sound of her footsteps, heavy in the still-too-big wellingtons, and Emmie stood to the side of the steps to let him go. She had given up chasing him, but she wanted to sit by the water and think about what had just happened. Why should she be the one to run away?

Jack stopped at the bottom of the steps, looking up at her. He had the model Hurricane that David had sent him for Christmas in his hands – he almost always did. Emmie thought he carried it around with him like a talisman. She wondered if he pretended to himself that it was David's plane. Something deep inside Jack prayed that the fragile metal shell thousands of feet up would be protected if its tiny model was safe. The plane was wooden, made by one of the other pilots in the squadron. David had written that he'd asked the man to build the plane for Jack, and paint it with the same camouflage pattern as David's own. The paint was rubbing away now, from so much holding, the sharp lines of the brown and khaki paint smoothing into each other.

"They won't let him come home."

Emmie gaped at him. It had been days and days

since he'd spoken to her, she had simply assumed that he would shove past her with a furious glare, as he had before. She was so surprised that for a moment she thought he was talking about his father, and she didn't know what to say. Then she saw the way he was cradling the plane.

"Your brother?"

"Mmm. He was hoping to get compassionate leave." His shoulders stiffened and hunched up. "Because of Dad."

"Oh. . ." She looked at him cautiously, wondering if he was still in that state where if someone was nice to him he would cry, and hate them for it. "I'm really sorry."

"Mmm. What was your nightmare about?"

Emmie blinked at him – she had almost forgotten. "Oh!" She chewed her bottom lip. "It's stupid, you'll laugh. . ."

"I won't, I promise."

"It was only that I couldn't get into the garden. I could see it, and it looked so sunny and beautiful, but I was stuck in all these shadows." She shivered, remembering.

"I had a dream like that about Dad," Jack said, slowly. He sat down on the steps, and Emmie sat next to him. Lucy padded away to peer down into the water.

"You couldn't get to him?"

"Yes, and he needed me to pull him up out of the water, but I couldn't reach." He put his chin in his hands. "It wasn't like that, actually. Mum got the letter. It was a torpedo from a U-boat, but he didn't drown. The torpedo set off an explosion, and it killed Dad and the captain – they were on the bridge. Lots of sailors were killed too, but then everyone else was rescued by another destroyer. It's silly – Dad's ship had stopped to rescue survivors, and then they went and got hit themselves. If they hadn't stopped, he might still be all right." He moved his hands up so they covered his face. His voice was muffled, and Emmie shifted closer to hear. "The destroyer that rescued the crew from Dad's ship had to sink her. They couldn't tow her back, not with everything that was going on, and she was too badly damaged anyway. So they used the guns on her. Dad loved that ship. He went down with her."

Emmie swallowed. "That's what they do in books, isn't it? It's like a hero thing to do."

"But this was real."

"I know. Sorry." Emmie leaned against him

gently – it seemed easier for him to pull away if she did that. But he put his head down on her shoulder, and they sat, watching Lucy's tail beat on the stones as she imagined hunting fish.

Emmie stopped on the path outside the green-painted door. It was standing open behind the ivy – Jack's mother was in there. Emmie could hear her humming to herself.

"What's the matter?" Jack turned back to look at her. "She said you could go back in there. She doesn't mind, Emmie. She told me last night that she'd talked to you."

"It isn't that," Emmie muttered huskily. "I've got something – I need to go back and get something. I'll be back in a minute." She raced back through the shrubbery to the house, pounding up the stairs and into her room. Then she sat down on her bed, breathless and uncertain. She had to give the diaries back – they were Mary's. But Mary hadn't wanted them, had she? She'd forgotten all about them, probably. She was busy with everything else. The faded little books had been in that drawer for nearly thirty years. If Emmie gave them back, she'd have to admit that she'd read them.

But most importantly, if she gave them back, she wouldn't be able to read them again. Emmie opened the drawer, and ran her fingers over the worn covers regretfully. Mary from the diary was so like her. Emmie had imagined meeting her, talking with her – that grumpy, friendless girl torn away from everything she knew. Now she *had* met Mary, but she was no longer a girl. She couldn't talk to Mrs Craven about how lonely she'd been, or the way the garden had come to feel like home. Not the same way she would have talked to Mary from all those years ago.

Still. The diaries weren't hers. She stood up, and began to walk slowly back along the passageway, and down the stairs.

The sun was brighter than ever, and the heat hit her as soon as she stepped out of the heavy door on to the gravel path. Lucy came trotting towards her from among the yew trees, mewing loudly.

"Where have you been?" Emmie murmured, crouching down to stroke her. "I thought you were begging in the kitchens. Were you out mousing?" Lucy purred, and rubbed against Emmie's ankles, her black fur shining in the sun. She was glossier every day, even if there weren't that many scraps for her to eat. She had adopted Mrs Martin, and kept bringing her small furry presents, usually in the middle of breakfast.

"Come with me," Emmie said coaxingly. She made chirruping noises as she crunched over the gravel, and Lucy bounded in front of her, darting off every so often to chase invisible bees.

"What were you doing?" Jack demanded, running over as he saw her duck under the ivy and out into the sunny garden. "You were gone for ages."

"Like I said, I was getting something. For your mother." Emmie marched across the grass and thrust the little pile of notebooks at Mrs Craven, who was deadheading roses. She blinked down at them in confusion.

"What are— Oh! Emmie, I'd forgotten these…" she murmured at last, turning the thin books over in her hands. "Of course, you're sleeping in my old room."

"I found them," Emmie admitted. "And I read them. I'm sorry. I didn't know – it seemed like such a long time ago. I never thought she was you."

Mary flicked through the pages, frowning at her own spiky writing. "So this is where you found the story about the garden, and Colin and me? It wasn't that anyone told you?"

"I told her about Dad's mother haunting the garden," Jack put in, peering over his mother's arm at the diary. "Your writing's much worse than mine."

"Too many governesses gave up on me. I'm amazed you could read them, Emmie."

"You don't mind?" Emmie whispered worriedly. "I didn't know it was you – not even when Jack said about his grandmother being a ghost. I didn't understand that it was Colin's mother. Mary was always a girl, like me."

Mary shook her head slowly. "No. No, I don't think I mind. She seems a long way away, that girl. It's like Dickon said, I was a mean-tempered little thing. But I was so used to being on my own. All I had were servants who didn't like me because I had such spoilt ways. The garden changed everything. Well, you know that it did." She smiled at Emmie, and sat down on the grass to look more carefully at the diaries. Jack crouched next to her, and Mary patted the grass, telling Emmie to sit too.

"Why did you stop writing a diary?" Emmie asked, curling up beside them cautiously, waiting for Mrs Craven to change her mind and send her away.

"I didn't. But Colin's father – Uncle Archie, I called him – gave me a beautiful new diary as a present. Red leather, with a lock, and a little golden key. I wore the key on a ribbon around my neck, it felt so special. Another secret. I wanted to write in that book instead, and I abandoned these. I wrote a diary all the way until the end of the war – the last war. And then I stopped. . ." She sighed. "It was too hard to write about. Nothing like that had happened to us before – Misselthwaite was so quiet. We were protected from everything. The war broke into that – even into the garden."

"Dickon had to go and fight," Emmie whispered. "And Colin."

"Yes. Colin had been away before, to go to school, but Dickon had hardly been off the moor." Mary shuddered. "It was … unbelievable. But we thought at least it could never happen again." She began to turn over the pages, tracing a word with her finger here and there.

Jack huddled against her, and Emmie stared at the grass. They sat silently, listening to the birds, until at last Mary pointed to the page she was reading. "So much of the garden is the same. Look, that rose is still here. The dark red one. I'm sure it still has the sweetest scent of them all." She smiled at Emmie. "Dickon cut some of those, you know. He gave them to your Miss Rose."

"Did he?" Emmie's eyes widened. "Yes! She had them in a vase in the schoolroom." She thought back, trying to remember if Miss Rose had said anything about the flowers. "Does that mean – if he's courting her – would she stay here, when we go back?"

Jack sat up straight, staring at her. "You're going back? When?"

"I don't know – I mean, when the war ends. Lots of children went back already, didn't they?" Emmie tried to look as though she didn't care. "No one's said."

Mary folded the diary closed, and slipped an arm around her shoulders. "I don't think the war is even nearly over, and it isn't safe for you children to be in London. You won't be going back for a long while."

"You promise you'd tell us?" Emmie begged. She wasn't sure she could bear to be dragged back again, back to sitting on a fire escape, and staring at the sky.

"I promise."

Chapter Nine

"Are those German?" Emmie asked anxiously, peering up at the sky.

"Yes!" Arthur said disgustedly. "Those are bombers. Junkers Ju 88, can't you tell?"

"No, I can't, you've got the binoculars. Can't I look?"

"You can see it without the binoculars," Jack pointed out. "Two massive engines – if they were Lancasters you'd see four little ones. I suppose you could mix them up with Whitleys." His voice implied that maybe Emmie could, but he certainly couldn't. "But they don't have those little tail fins. And anyway, Emmie, these have got black crosses painted on, see? Under the wings and at the back of the fuselage."

"I think I can see." Emmie squinted up at the planes, black and menacing against the sunlight. The droning buzz of the engines sounded sinister, but perhaps that was only because she knew they were the enemy. "Do you reckon they're going to Linton, then?"

"Might be. Or Driffield. Here, give me a go with those." Joey grabbed the binoculars off Arthur, who pulled a face, but didn't say anything. It had been Joey who found the binoculars in the gun room, and he had first claim.

They'd heard the drone of the bombers overhead just as they were putting away their books, and they'd all hurtled out on to the terrace, where there was a good view.

"It looks like hundreds of them," Emmie murmured.

"Nope. Fifty or so." Arthur had his hands up, shielding his eyes from the sun. "I've never seen that many."

"God help the poor blighters wherever they are going. . ." Joey muttered. "Fifty? You're sure?"

Arthur shrugged. "Maybe more. Heavy bombers."

"I suppose they know, at Driffield. . ." Jack murmured. "They'll have been spotted coming over, won't they?"

"Must have been." Joey lowered the binoculars. "Bet they've scrambled fighters from Leconfield already."

The drone was fading away now, the last of the heavy dark planes disappearing across the moor.

"They're gone," Arthur sighed. "I wish we could have seen a dogfight."

Jack shuddered, but he didn't say anything, just slipped his hand into the pocket of his shorts. Emmie knew he had the wooden Hurricane in there, his talisman.

There were planes overhead almost every day now, if it was good weather. Fighting weather. Since the beginning of July, the German Luftwaffe had been dropping bombs on the ships sailing in convoy in the English Channel. The Germans had attacked the merchant ships so fiercely that now they only sailed at night. They had bombed the naval bases and harbours heavily too, and the manufacturing towns, where many of the weapons factories were. The first daylight raid of the war had come in early July, on the massive oil storage tanks at Hull, which even Emmie knew was in Yorkshire. The RAF couldn't fly their planes without fuel.

Jack's brother David was flying from an airbase

in Suffolk now. Jack kept scanning the newspapers, looking for anything about the air battles. There were so many accounts of planes shot down – from the RAF and the Luftwaffe. The day before Emmie had snatched the paper off him, because his hands were shaking.

"I wonder if they dropped any parachutists?" Joey was still gazing out across the moor.

"We'd have seen." Jack turned back, looking up too.

"They found parachutes near Leeds," Joey reminded him stubbornly. "That was only yesterday."

"We know!" Emmie sighed. "You haven't stopped going on about it since."

"Well, there could be spies camping out on the moor for all we know." Joey adjusted the focus on the binoculars again.

"What would they want to do that for?" Jack frowned at him. "What could they report back – how the heather's flowering?"

"This is talking about the day before yesterday," Emmie murmured, clutching the newspaper that Jack had stuffed into her hands. "The day we saw all those German planes flying over the moor."

"It was a huge attack," Jack said huskily. He dropped down next to her under the tree. "There were hundreds of them. The ones we saw wiped out Great Driffield – all the hangars got flattened. They bombed the Whitleys standing on the airfield, blew them all up. There were a load more of them fighting over Sunderland, but there were attacks down south as well. There are more attacks every day now. Hitler's trying to wipe out our RAF, so he can invade. That's what it says in here." He stabbed a finger at the newspaper. "David's squadron would have been fighting too, they'd have flown out from Martlesham. It's 11 Group that's really taking the pressure, this says. That's the squadrons in the south-east. That's him."

"He has to be safe," Emmie whispered. "It wouldn't be fair. Not both of them. Not him and your dad."

"I don't think anything's fair any more." Jack swallowed.

Emmie smoothed the paper down over her skirt. "Does your mother knew you're reading the newspapers?" she asked suddenly.

Jack shrugged and turned his head away, and Emmie knew that meant no. "This is Mrs Martin's paper, isn't it? You swiped it from the kitchen."

"Mum won't let me see hers any more," Jack said flatly. Then he looked back at Emmie and began to gabble, as though the words were pouring out of him without permission. "They don't want me to know what it's like, her and Miss Sowerby! They think I'm too young to understand. So all I get is Joey and Arthur taking it in turns to be the *Huns* and racing round shooting each other down. Spouting about *kills* and *strafing*, and *bailing out*..." He stopped, gasping for breath. "David isn't telling me the truth either – he's stopped saying anything useful in his letters. I know they're not allowed to say much because of the censor reading their post, but he used to write me proper letters, long ones, with funny stories in about buzzing over sheep in fields, or spilling soup all down his front when they had to scramble. Now all he says is he's all right, and lots of love, and look after Mum."

"Maybe he's just tired," Emmie suggested.

"I don't want him to be tired! He's got to fly! They've got seconds to spot the enemy aircraft, just seconds, Emmie! He can't even blink. He can't be tired." Jack dragged the wooden plane out of his pocket. "Lot of use this is going to be..." He laughed shakily, and Emmie looked at him sideways. His eyes had a strange, eerie glitter to them, and they looked huger than ever. He didn't look like his brother at all, Emmie thought vaguely. Jack was so like his father, with those great black-lashed grey eyes, and David was tall, with thick brown hair like his mother's.

Emmie tried not to let herself shiver – Jack was sitting close enough to feel it if she did. But she could picture Jack's brother so clearly that it felt almost as if she knew him too. Jack had a photograph of David in his RAF uniform by his bed, Emmie had looked at it often. It was strange how that one moment staring into the camera had caught so much about him. She knew how excited he was about becoming a pilot. How everything was a great joke, even being up in the air with nothing but a sheet of thin metal between him and the sky, and the guns. She knew how much Jack loved him.

It wasn't just the photograph, of course. Emmie had all the stories, everything Jack had told her. All those strange little moments that reminded him of his adored big brother. Even the garden made Jack think of hide and seek, or David laughing and swinging him round and round in the middle of the grass. It was like flying, David had said, that was what flying felt like... They'd gone so fast he got dizzy, and they fell over and lay on the grass together laughing.

Jack gripped the plane in his hands so tightly that Emmie heard it splinter.

"Be careful! You'll break it!"

But he jumped up, shoving it angrily back into his pocket. Then he grabbed her arm and pulled her after him out of the garden.

"Where are we going?"

"Down by the sheds. Dickon had a bonfire this morning, didn't he? He was burning leaves, I smelled them." He raced her through the kitchen gardens, and out to the strip of ground between the gardens and the wood, where the gardeners' tool sheds were, and the compost heaps, and a patch of ashy ground for bonfires. Jack crouched down by the cindery mess, and nodded. "Look, I thought so. There's still embers there." He stirred them with a stick, and blew, puffing out his cheeks so that a tiny flame licked up. "Emmie, help me get some of the dry stuff out of that barrow. Dickon didn't have time to burn it all, look." He seized an armful of garden trimmings, and cast them on the fire, still blowing. The green branches frazzled and wisped sharp-smelling smoke, but the dry grass and weeds crisped grey at once, and the flames rose a little higher. Doubtfully, Emmie threw on another load. She loved watching the bonfires, but she wasn't sure this stuff was properly ready to burn. And the set look on Jack's face was frightening her.

"We're not supposed to. . ." she started to say. But then she gave up. Jack didn't care. And today, she wasn't sure anyone else would, either.

"That's good enough," Jack muttered, looking at the flames. There was still a lot of sullen smoke, but the fire had a glowing orange heart, criss-crossed with burned twigs.

He pulled out the plane David had sent him again, and rubbed his fingers over the worn paint. He muttered something.

"What?" Emmie leaned closer, coughing a little as the smoke caught in her throat.

"I said, it isn't going to work." Jack looked round at her. "It was supposed to keep him safe. How can it? It's just a toy, Emmie! It can't do anything! He's going to die. Just like Dad. . ." He turned back to the fire, and before Emmie realized what he was doing, he crouched down and shoved the tiny plane into the crackling centre. Then he stepped back, his eyes full of tears, cradling his burned hand.

"You can't do that!" Emmie screamed. "He gave it to you! Get it out!"

Jack shook his head. "It isn't going to work... I can't have it any more, it makes me think about him too much. It hurts." He stared blindly at the fire, and stumbled away, leaving Emmie hovering at the edge of the fire.

"You mustn't do that," Emmie wept. The little aeroplane was charred already, its faded paint blackened. A few moments more and it would be gone. Emmie kicked at the fire with her boots, tearing apart the seething, spitting weeds. She grabbed a stick, and hooked the burning toy out – it was half gone already, one wing hardly there at all. Emmie ran to the water butt by the tool shed, and seized a dipper of water. She flung it down on the plane, and it hissed, little cracks opening up along the wood. Sighing, she squatted down to look at it. The plane was ruined – hardly recognizable. But she picked it up anyway, folding it carefully in her handkerchief.

Even if Jack couldn't bear to look at it any more, she would keep it. Someone had to remember, and hope.

Chapter Ten

"Emmie. Emmie. I don't like it. It's shrieking at me. You've been so long washing." Ruby was huddled in a ball in the corner of her bed, but as Emmie came into the bedroom, the little girl sprang up and ran at her. She clung on tight, with her arms around Emmie's middle.

"It's only the wind," Emmie said, half-laughing. But she could feel Ruby shaking. She remembered being frightened by the crying of the wind in the chimney herself, and realized with surprise that that had only been a year before. "I suppose you want to get in my bed then?"

Ruby nodded into Emmie's chest, but she didn't move, and she wouldn't let go. Emmie had to walk her over to the bed, and sit down with her.

"I have to get my nightdress on, Ruby. Get in. Look, I won't go anywhere, I promise. Hide under the covers. Lucy'll sit on you." She reached out round the littler girl to pull the blankets back, and Ruby hurled herself underneath them, burying her head under the pillow so that only the dark ends of her hair trailed out. Lucy pawed at it curiously, and then tried clawing Ruby's arm. Ruby didn't come out from the pillow, she just scooped Lucy in and pulled the blankets up over both of them.

Emmie tried not to laugh. Ruby was big enough now to hate it when she thought people were laughing at her. She changed into her nightie, and nudged Ruby over, wondering if once Ruby was asleep she could go and sleep in Ruby's bed. Two girls and a cat was going to be a squash.

"Is it really only the wind?" Ruby whispered into Emmie's neck.

"It's just the way the wind blows round the chimney, Ruby, honestly. I was scared of it too, when we first came here. I've heard it before, and nothing ever happened to me, did it?"

"I suppose."

Emmie leaned back against the pillow, shifting a little to get herself comfortable between Ruby and the cat. The rain lashed across the windows, rattling the glass. Emmie turned her head so she could see the tapestries, smiling at the white horse with the long, foolish nose – her favourite. The wind howled again, but Ruby only twitched a little. She was almost asleep. Emmie sighed. If they'd still been in London, it would be the air-raid sirens wailing like that. Mrs Evans had told them, when she came back from visiting her sister. The wind in the chimney sounded almost friendly, especially when the room was warm, and Lucy had climbed out from under the blankets to purr by the pillow.

Emmie was almost asleep herself when she heard the door squeaking, a sharp, real noise, very different to the crying of the wind. Her heart thudded, even though she knew it couldn't be burglars, or anything like that. It was just that it was late, and deep down she couldn't help it… She sat up on one elbow, gasping in a deep breath and hoping it wasn't Miss Rose or Miss Dearlove. They were sure to make Ruby move, and then she'd cry, and Emmie almost didn't mind her being there.

"Oh, it's you! Ssshhh, don't wake her."

Jack slid in round the door, his torch, his precious Christmas present, pointed down at the floor. "I couldn't sleep." He perched on the end of the bed and looked at Emmie sideways, a bit shifty. "It's really loud in my room. Much louder than here, the rain really smashes against the window. I couldn't sleep. And I thought maybe you'd be awake too."

"I was only half-asleep." Emmie yawned. "Ruby had a panic. I don't know what she thought the wind was – ghosts probably." She grinned at him. "For half a second I thought you were one, or a murderer. It's that sort of night."

Jack nodded. "It is... Everything feels funny being up so late, doesn't it? Knowing everyone else is asleep. It changes things."

"What things?" Emmie blinked at him tiredly.

Jack shrugged, and then turned to look at her. "Perhaps it makes it easier to talk. David used to let me talk to him, if I woke up in the night. I think he was asleep a lot of the time though. All he did was grunt, mostly."

Emmie giggled. "I could do that..."

"I really, really miss him. I burned his plane, Emmie. Why did I do something that stupid? He gave it to me."

Emmie sighed, and wriggled further away from Ruby so she could reach over to the bedside table. "You owe me a handkerchief," she murmured. "Miss Dearlove moaned at me for ages." She pulled the sad little parcel out, and handed it to him. "It's not all there. A wing's gone. And the paint's sort of bubbled off."

Jack gaped at the plane, charred and broken in his hands, and then at Emmie. "You pulled it out? Why didn't you tell me?"

"Because you'd have gone and put it straight back in, of course! I was waiting till I thought you'd want it. Sorry. Maybe I should have given it back to you before. But you still seemed … not ready for it."

Jack hunched up one shoulder at her, half-shrug, half-nod. "Maybe you're right," he muttered. He sighed, slow and shaky. "If she's in your bed, can I sleep in hers? No one'll mind."

Privately Emmie reckoned Miss Dearlove would, but she didn't care. "Go on then. Don't blame me if Ruby jumps on you in the middle of the night and has a screaming fit, though."

"It *is* the middle of the night."

"Shut up and go to sleep then." Emmie wriggled

back down, curling herself around Ruby, and smiling in the dark. The plane had been haunting her, from inside that drawer. It still belonged to Jack, she'd felt as if it wanted to go back to him. She peered across the room to the shadowy lump under the window. There was a hint of whiteness pressed against his face – her handkerchief, still wrapped around the plane.

Emmie surfaced slowly from the grey dream again. It came every so often, that terrible sense of longing and despair as she was shut away from the garden. She clenched her hands on the blankets, breathing fast. It wasn't real. Just a dream. "Only a dream," she muttered, repeating it to herself like a chant. "Only a dream."

Ruby huffed and wriggled and mewed like a kitten, and went back to sleep. Emmie sat up, rubbing at her arms.

"You're awake." Jack was kneeling up on Ruby's bed, looking out of the window. "It's getting light."

"So it is." It must be, she could properly see him. She slid out of bed, and went to stand next to him at the window. He'd opened it, she noticed. The smell of rain-wet garden eased around her, and she took a deep breath in, banishing the dream. "Shall we go out?" she asked suddenly.

Jack looked round at her. "Now?"

"Why not? You could put Arthur's boots on – they're by the side door." Emmie stood on tiptoe, resting her elbows on the windowsill. "I want to be out in it. I want to see the sun come up."

Jack scrambled off the bed, tucking the wrapped plane into the pocket of his too-small dressing gown, and Emmie snatched the blanket off Ruby's bed. They crept out of the room and along the passage and down the stairs, pale and ghostly in the pre-dawn light.

The bolts were stiff, and shrieked. They stared at each other, round-eyed and frozen by the door, but no one came after them. Jack yanked the door open, and grabbed her hand, and they went running out through the gardens. There was a faint pinkness at the lower edges of the sky, and the fish pond glimmered in the light of Jack's torch as they raced past.

The ivy rustled as Emmie reached for the handle, and the door shushed over the grass. The garden was full of birds, calling to each other as the children crept in. Emmie wanted to dance about on the wet grass, but she didn't – the garden wasn't theirs so early, they were visitors. They huddled next to each other on the bench, watching the trees and the statue and the sundial grow clearer and sharper as the darkness seeped out of the sky. Jack held the wooden plane in both hands, cradling it like a tiny bird.

A faint September mist swirled around their feet, and the birdsong faded to a chirrup, here and there. Emmie thought she saw the robin, perched in the rose arch overhead and peering down at them with curious bead eyes. But the light wasn't good enough to be sure.

"The sun's coming up," Jack whispered. "I've never seen it from outside before. It feels like magic. The sky's turned golden. I can feel everything in the garden; it's all reaching up for the light."

"Someone's coming," Emmie whispered, clutching at his hand. "Jack, someone's coming, I can hear footsteps on the path. The door!"

It was probably only Dickon – or perhaps Jack's mother, come to look for him. But in the early morning light, there was a breathless sense of something about to happen. Something strange, or frightening, or wonderful, Emmie couldn't tell which. Perhaps all of them at once.

The door shifted a little, and then drew open, and a tall figure stepped through, out of the shadows.

"Who is it?" Emmie asked, her voice gone high and squeaky. But Jack was already gone, the little wooden plane and the handkerchief had slipped on to the bench. He was laughing and laughing, running across the grass towards his brother.

Emmie Hatton
Misselthwaite Manor
29th October 1940

Mrs Craven gave me back the diaries. She said that she had loved reading them again, but now she thought I wanted them more than she did. She gave me a pencil too, a pretty one with a striped paper wrapper around it. She showed me the end of the diary, and the empty pages, and even though she didn't say so, I know she meant for me to write in them myself. But I didn't know how to begin. I hadn't anything to write about, except that we have been here for a year. More than a year, now it's October. I wanted my diary to start with something special. I wanted something to happen, and now it has.

The Home has been bombed. Miss Dearlove told us this morning. It just isn't there any more, nothing is left at all. It wasn't just the Home, the bombs destroyed most of the street — but no one was killed, everyone had gone to the shelters. She was shaking when she said it, and I suppose I ought to be shocked too. But London seems so far away. I almost can't remember the me that lived there.

We can never, ever go back. Mrs Craven explained it to all of us, that the Home will be at Misselthwaite for

always, not just while the war is on. She promised.
That means that we belong here now.

An Interview with Holly Webb

What made you want to write a sequel to *The Secret Garden*?

It's one of my favourite-ever books. I wish I still had the copy I had as a child – it was dark blue leather, with a portrait of Mary set into the cover, looking very pale and sickly! I loved the characters, but particularly Misselthwaite Manor itself. The idea of continuing on the story of the house and the garden was so tempting.

Have you ever written a sequel before? What was the biggest challenge?

No, I haven't, though I have read sequels to some of my

favourite books. That was one of the things that worried me, actually – I'd been so cross about some parts of those sequels that to me seemed so obviously "wrong"! What if someone else felt the same way about my book? I could just imagine all the furious letters – especially about some parts of the plot, and what happens to certain people…

Did you feel any sort of responsibility towards Frances Hodgson Burnett's characters?

Yes. If you've read the book and you aren't just skipping to the end (tch!) you'll know that even though Emmie and her contemporaries aren't from the original book, several of the other characters are. I loved those characters, and it felt a huge privilege to be allowed to imagine what happened to them next. I'm still a bit worried about what I've done to them though…

Did you find it easy to imagine the children from the original as grown-ups?

Yes and no. As I reread The Secret Garden *as an older child (I reread my favourite books a lot) and thought about when it was written, it became obvious to me that* the children, Mary, Colin and Dickon, were growing up just before the First World War. Colin and Dickon would have been expected to fight. Colin grows up in the book and gets well, and might have gone off to boarding school, but Dickon probably wouldn't ever have left the moor. Imagine going from such a small, well-known world to fighting in France. It would have had an indescribable effect on him. It was quite hard to imagine the transformation of such a loving, happy child.

Return to the Secret Garden is set during the Second World War. How did you keep the story historically accurate?

I had several excellent reference books: Wartime: Britain 1939-1945 by Juliet Gardiner was my main reference – it's full of letters and documents, and is really interesting. I also read The People's War by Angus Calder, and Doodlebugs, Gasmasks and Gum by Christina Rex – that's a collection of interviews about people's wartime experiences as children. I also used a lot of online references – all sorts of things such as the London Transport Museum archives for details about trains and stations, histories of various RAF bases, and the BBC Archive, which was wonderful. I spent one *whole afternoon listening to radio broadcasts about evacuees, and crying. One of the interviewers asked all the children on the platform to cheer – they had no idea what was happening, or even where they were going, but they still did. I have a horrible feeling that there are mistakes, though, all of which are down to me.*

What about the garden itself? Are you a keen gardener, or did this require some research too?

I love gardening, but I'm not hugely good at it… One of my favourite parts of The Secret Garden *is Frances Hodgson Burnett's evident love of the garden she created. She actually based it on a house where she lived a few years before she wrote the book: Great Maytham Hall in Kent, where there was a real walled garden, though I don't think it was ever as neglected and abandoned as the garden at Misselthwaite. The trickiest bit was trying to map the gardens from the descriptions she gives. I'm terrible at spatial awareness, and I wanted to have a sense of where things really were, but it was so hard to pin down!*

Do you have a favourite character or moment from the original book?

Definitely Mary. But I have to admit that I prefer her about halfway through the book, before she reforms entirely and becomes a lot less grumpy and stubborn. I adore Colin, but by the end of the story, I can't help thinking that Mary lets him boss her about far too much! The main characters in Frances Hodgson Burnett's other two most well-known novels, A Little Princess *and* Little Lord Fauntleroy, *are annoyingly saintly (particularly Cecil, Lord Fauntleroy), but Mary Lennox always seemed much more likely to me! I also loved* The Painted Garden *by Noel Streatfeild, who's best-known for writing* Ballet Shoes. The Painted Garden *is about a girl cast as Mary in a film of* The Secret Garden. *I'd recommend it – Jane is equally deliciously bad-tempered…*

My favourite moment from the original story is when the robin shows Mary the knob of the door, and she first gets into the garden. I had to put a robin in my book too.

Visit Holly's website at holly-webb.com